SEAS OF SOUTH AFRICA

OTHER BOOKS BY PHILIP ROY

*Me & Mr. Bell* (2013)

*Outlaw in India* (2012)

*Blood Brothers in Louisbourg* (2012)

*Ghosts of the Pacific* (2011)

*River Odyssey* (2010)

*Journey to Atlantis* (2009)

*Submarine Outlaw* (2008)

# Seas of
# South Africa

*For Julia R.*

*Wonderous voyage!*

Philip Roy

RONSDALE PRESS

SEAS OF SOUTH AFRICA
Copyright © 2013 Philip Roy

RONSDALE PRESS
3350 West 21st Avenue, Vancouver, B.C., Canada V6S 1G7
www.ronsdalepress.com

Typesetting: Julie Cochrane, in Minion 12 pt on 16
Cover Art & Design: Nancy de Brouwer, Massive Graphic Design
Map: Veronica Hatch & Julie Cochrane
Paper: Ancient Forest Friendly "Silva" (FSC)—100% post-consumer waste,
    totally chlorine-free and acid-free

Ronsdale Press wishes to thank the following for their support of its publishing program: the Canada Council for the Arts, the Government of Canada through the Canada Book Fund, the British Columbia Arts Council and the Province of British Columbia through the British Columbia Book Publishing Tax Credit program.

Library and Archives Canada Cataloguing in Publication

Roy, Philip, 1960–, author
    Seas of South Africa / Philip Roy.

Issued in print and electronic formats.
ISBN 978-1-55380-247-1 (print)
ISBN 978-1-55380-248-8 (ebook) / ISBN 978-1-55380-249-5 (pdf)

    I. Title.

PS8635.O91144S42 2013     jC813'.6     C2013-903172-3     C2013-903173-1

At Ronsdale Press we are committed to protecting the environment. To this end we are working with Canopy (formerly Markets Initiative) and printers to phase out our use of paper produced from ancient forests. This book is one step towards that goal.

Printed in Canada by Marquis Printing, Quebec

*for Julian*

## ACKNOWLEDGEMENTS

Many thanks to the readers of the *Submarine Outlaw* series, those that we meet in schools, and those at home who write us letters. We greatly appreciate the feedback and suggestions. Thanks once again to Ron and Veronica at Ronsdale for guiding my course, and also to Deirdre, Maria, and Julie. Thanks again to Nancy for her wonderful covers.

It is a pleasure to acknowledge the people who inspire and support me on a daily basis: my wife Leila (and furry Fritzi); my kids, Julia, Peter, Thomas (and partner, Lydia), and Julian; my mother, Ellen; my sister, Angela; and my dearest friends, Chris, Natasha, and Chiara. Thanks also to Zaan and Nicholas, for your friendship and hospitality in South Africa.

"*I asked myself what I was doing there,
with a sensation of panic in my heart
as though I had blundered into a place
of cruel and absurd mysteries . . .*"

— JOSEPH CONRAD, *Heart of Darkness*

"*But there comes a time, as it came in
my life, when a man is denied the right to live
a normal life, when he can only live the life of an
outlaw because the government has so decreed to use
the law to impose a life of outlawry upon him.*"

— NELSON MANDELA, *Long Walk to Freedom*

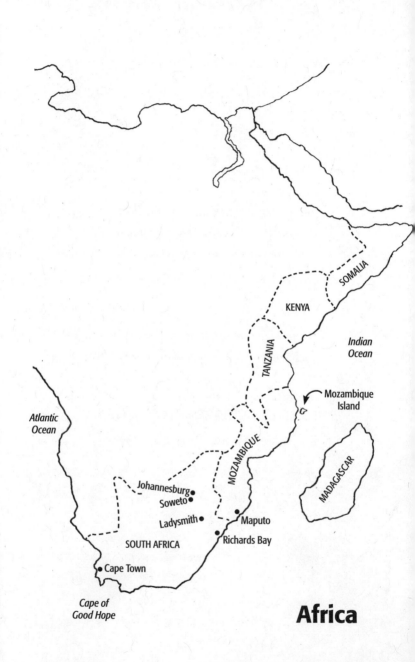

**Africa**

# Chapter One

∞

I HAVE LEARNED THAT you cannot pick and choose what you will find when you go out to explore. Sometimes you will find beautiful things, and sometimes you will find ugly things. That is the world we live in. In South Africa, where the warm Indian Ocean meets the cold Atlantic, like a meeting of two tigers, and where the hearts of people seem both bigger and darker than anywhere else, I found both.

This journey really started seven months ago when I left Newfoundland in my twenty-five foot submarine, with Hollie and Seaweed, my dog and seagull crew. Since then, we've been across the Arctic, down and around the Pacific, over to India, and across the Indian Ocean to Mozambique, on the southeast coast of Africa, where we were now. I had wondered if sailing the world this way would make it seem smaller, but it has been the opposite. It is impossible to describe how big our world really is, how unlike each part is from the others, and how different the animals and people are—the whales, turtles, monkeys, snakes, dolphins, polar bears, fieldworkers, Inuit, fishermen, street beggars . . . And yet, none of that prepared me for what we would discover in the seas of South Africa.

I was sitting in a barber's chair when he walked in the door. The barbershop looked like it was made of tin. It sat between an old chandlery and a dry goods store with broken windows and cobwebs across the front door. The street was dusty and unpaved, and reminded me of ghost towns in old movie westerns. The street was perched above a crooked pier in an old corner of Porto Amélia, Mozambique, and looked like it would slide into the sea if the wind ever blew here, which it didn't seem likely to do. Maybe it had once been a busy corner of town, but it appeared abandoned now. It wasn't.

I had moored the sub beneath the pier because the pier was falling apart, and I thought nobody would be in the shacks above it. But I was wrong. There was a small man with tiny curls on his head and face, like pig's hair, and he jumped to his feet as soon as I walked past his window. He held a pair of scissors in his hand, and stabbed them at me. "'air cut?" he said. He looked so hopeful.

I reached up to touch my hair. It fell down over my ears and onto my shoulder. I probably looked like a girl. I studied the old man's face carefully. He looked honest and trustworthy. Maybe it was a good idea. "Sure! Why not?" So, I came into his shop and sat down in the first chair. "No, no," he said. "'ere!" So, I got up and followed him around the corner into a tiny room that was hanging right over the water. There was another man sleeping in the chair. The first man said something in a clicking kind of language and slapped the sleeping man's knee. His bloodshot eyes opened wide, and he hopped out of the chair like a boy. When I sat down, the chair was warm. The first man pulled a rubber sheet off the wall and wrapped it over me. "I'd like . . ." I started to say, but he left the room. He came back with a sticky green bottle. "I'd like . . ." But the man was nodding his head as if I had already told him what I wanted, and I didn't think he was listening anymore. He poured a little liquid into his hands and rubbed them together. It smelled like licorice and shoe polish. He stood behind me and started rubbing my scalp with his fingers. I thought that was strange but figured it was probably what they did here before they cut your hair. I settled into my chair and started to feel sleepy. That's when he walked in the door.

Sometimes you meet someone and you know that they are bad. You don't know how you know, you just know. That's what I knew about this man right away. When he came into the shop, he barked loudly at the other barber and took a seat in one of the first chairs. Though I couldn't see him, I could see the barber every time he turned around to pick up something from his table. The first thing the barber did was fill a kettle with water and put it onto a hotplate hooked up to a generator. Then he picked up a straight razor and started sharpening it with a leather belt while he waited for the kettle to boil. And all of that time, the man in the chair barked words at him I didn't understand.

As I leaned back in my chair, I tried to figure out why I didn't like the man who had come in. I didn't even know him. Partly it was because he was so loud. He didn't just talk; he shouted. Then, he was also disrespectful to the barber, even though I couldn't understand what he was saying. I could tell by the sound of his voice. The barber was a quiet and gentle man. He didn't deserve to be treated like that.

But there was something else in the stranger's energy, something darker, or violent. I could feel it, and it made me uncomfortable. He sounded like somebody who had spent all of his life in bad company. Was he a hardened criminal who had just been released from prison? Was he a pirate? I had read about the pirates of Somalia, and had seen them on TV. But they were younger than him. Some were just my age, sixteen or seventeen. He was a lot older than that. I could tell by his voice. And he had come in alone. Somali pirates travelled in packs. They cruised offshore in small boats, attacked passing sailboats, yachts, and cruise ships; climbed onto freighters and tankers, took their crews hostage, and demanded ransom. They kidnapped people and held them hostage for months, even years, until they were paid millions of dollars in ransom. They killed people, disrupted the shipping industry, and cast a dark shadow over the east coast of Africa. They were making the sea an ugly place. I hated them for that.

But this was Mozambique. Somalia was over a thousand miles north. And I had made a promise to Ziegfried that I wouldn't sail within five hundred miles of it. And I hadn't. Otherwise, he would have dry-docked my sub back in India, which was his right since he had built it in the first place and was dedicated to my safety. I had promised to agree to that if he felt it was no longer safe. He was like a father to me. I had to listen to him.

When the kettle boiled, the barber poured the boiling water into a wooden bowl. He dipped a shaving brush into the bowl and lathered up a block of soap. His movements were shaky, and I wondered if he was afraid. I could understand why. The man in the chair was barking at him, and then, suddenly, he stopped. He asked him a one-word question. The barber didn't answer. Then the man burst out in English. "You weren't listening to me! You didn't understand a word I said, did you, you little *kaaaf*?" The barber's head dropped a little, and he paused for a second. The barber rubbing my head paused too. Then the other barber picked up the brush and started lathering the man's face.

"Shave close!" warned the man, "or I'll stick you on a spin-dle and feed you to the sharks! Hah, hah, hah, hah, hah, hah, hah . . ." He had a heavy accent that sounded European, but I was guessing he was probably from South Africa. He kept talking. He had the sound of someone who needed to talk because he spent so much time alone at sea. Here, on the edge of nowhere, he had to be coming from the sea.

I watched the barber rinse his brush in the bowl, put it down on the table and pick up the razor. As the razor swung through the air, a big ugly hand reached out and grabbed the barber's skinny arm and squeezed it. "Now, you keep that arm good and steady if you know what's good for you, hey?" The barber behind me stopped rubbing my scalp. He reached down and picked up a pair of scissors. He didn't make a sound. Our eyes met, and for a split second we looked at each other. I wondered what he was thinking, but couldn't tell. The next thing I heard was the sound of the razor scraping the man's throat. It sounded like someone opening a strip of Velcro slowly. I saw it swing through the air again and the barber wipe it clean with a cloth.

The barber behind me started cutting my hair. It dropped onto my lap and the floor, but I wasn't really paying atten-tion. I hoped the unfriendly man would finish first and leave. I was careful not to make a sound, and the barber cut my hair very quietly. I think he didn't want to be noticed, either. All of a sudden, the man yelled. "Ouch! You stupid . . . ! You miserable wretch! Watch what you're doing with that razor! You cut me again and I'll slice you into little pieces and hook you for bait! Hold your hand steady!"

I saw the razor swing back. The barber's hand was shaking. The barber behind me stopped cutting, put the scissors down and opened a drawer in the small desk beside me. He didn't make a sound. I saw a small grey handgun in the drawer. It looked like a toy. The barber dropped a face towel on top of the gun, covering it. Then he turned and smiled at me awkwardly. I forced a smile back. I wanted to get out of here.

The shave continued, and so did the man's talk. "I've been here before, to this place, a long time ago. A lot more people around then. Used to be a thriving place, when the Portuguese were here. Lots of wreck divers, mapmakers, sailors for hire, investigators . . . a lot of fancy names. Thought they were all better than me." He paused. "They were no better than me. They were just treasure hunters, too. Now they call themselves oceanographers, ecologists, environmentalists. Fancy names, aren't they? Baaaaaaah! They're no different than me." He raised his voice until he was almost shouting. "You think I'm a nobody?" Suddenly he lowered his voice to barely a whisper. "Well, I'll tell you something—you can't understand me anyway, can you?—those guys don't know a real treasure from a bag of rocks. But I do. I do because I've got one." He raised his voice again. "There! Put that in your pipe and smoke it! Hah!"

The barber dipped a face towel into the bowl, wrung it out

and handed it to the man. He reached for a bottle next. "No. Don't put that stink on me! I've got plenty good smell all my own. Hah!"

I heard him get up. The shop shook under his weight. His hand slapped a bill down on the barber's table. "There! Buy yourself a shave! Hah, hah, hah!" I hoped he would leave now. I held my breath. But the barber beside me reached for the scissors again, missed them, and they fell to the floor. Shoot! The man took a few heavy steps . . . and there he was.

His face looked like it had been beaten with a shovel. It had scars and bumps all over it. His nose was twisted, his teeth were yellow and brown, and mostly broken, and one side of his face was bigger than the other. His eyes were big and bloodshot, his head was big; *everything* about him was big. On his head he wore a captain's cap with holes in it, which looked about fifty years old. I couldn't help thinking he would make a good model for a Halloween mask.

He was surprised to see us there, as I thought he would be. He stood and glared suspiciously. "You look like an English boy," he said accusingly.

I didn't want to answer him, but I had to say something. "Canada."

"Canada?" He looked confused. "What are you doing here? How'd you get here? Come overland? I didn't see a jeep outside. Where are your parents? You must have sailed here. But I didn't see a boat. How'd you get here?"

He stood there with a scowl on his face, like a bully. The

barber behind me took a small step towards the desk. I hoped he didn't reach for the gun. That little pea-shooter probably wouldn't even stop the man; it might only make him angry. I tried to tell him as little as possible. "I sailed here."

"You sailed here? With who?"

That was none of his business. Who the heck did he think he was? "By myself."

He looked like he didn't believe me. "Then where's your boat? I never saw a boat."

"It's down the shore a little ways. What difference does it make?" I tried to sound tougher than I felt because I knew you have to stand up to a bully. But he was so much bigger than me, and he looked really dangerous. He just stared at me for a while, as if he were trying to make up his mind. I tried to look like I didn't care about anything. Finally, he just snickered with disgust, turned around, and walked out the door. But he didn't go far. We all listened to his footsteps. The other barber stuck his face around the corner, looked at us and shook his head.

I took a deep breath. I had been holding my breath for a long time. The barber continued cutting my hair. He cut slowly. I figured he was trying to take a long time so the man would leave the area before I went outside. That suited me fine until I realized I didn't have any hair left. And then the barber picked up a small battery-powered razor and shaved the rest of my head! I put my hand on top of my head and it felt like sandpaper. I looked down at the floor and saw all of my hair lying there like rabbit fur. Then the barber held a mirror up behind my head. I was bald! Ah, well, I probably *had* looked like a girl. I rubbed my head again. It actually felt kind of good. It was nice and cool. I stood up. "How much do I owe you?"

The barber clicked like he was swallowing something. "Five dollar."

I reached into my pocket and gave him a wrinkled American five dollar bill. He nodded his head. Then he picked up the little grey gun and offered it to me. I stared at it. It was probably a lot more dangerous than I first thought it was. "No, thank you," I said. "I'll be okay." I shook hands with both of the barbers and said goodbye.

When I stepped outside, he was waiting for me.

# Chapter Two

HE WRAPPED AN ARM around me in a way that was supposed to be friendly but wasn't, and I hated it. He squeezed me tight so that he could pull me along in his direction. I didn't try to free myself because that might start a fight between us, and I wasn't ready for that. He'd probably kill me. So, I went along with him for the moment, but waited for my chance to escape. It was really awkward and uncomfortable. And he stank.

He pulled me towards the end of the street, from where we could see the water below. It was about thirty feet down. There was only one boat there, a sailboat. And it must have been his, because there hadn't been one when I sailed in. My sub was there, too, but you couldn't see it because it was in the shadows under the pier. He stopped when we were facing the water and pointed with his head. "So, where's your boat?"

"I told you, it's down the shore a ways."

"Oh, I see. Down the shore?"

"Yah."

"Well, isn't that funny? I just sailed *up* the shore, and I never saw a sailboat. Do you suppose it sank?"

"It's there. How else do you think I got here?"

"Well, that's what I'm trying to figure out. And you heard me talking in there, didn't you?"

"I wasn't listening."

"You weren't listening? That's a good one. A man talks about treasure, and you're not listening? You're a crafty one, my boy. Now, tell me a little about your boat. It must be a motorboat then, is it, because I never saw a sail, and I was looking. If there was a sail, I'd have seen it. But I could've missed a motorboat. Maybe you moored it in the shallows, did you? How long is it?"

His arm was so strong it was like getting pinned against the wall by a horse. "It's twenty-five feet."

"A twenty-five foot motorboat? Now we're getting somewhere. It must be fast then, is it?"

"It's fast enough."

"I'll bet it is. It'll be a heck of a lot faster than what I'm sailing right now. Maybe we should trade."

"I'm not interested in trading."

"Oh, you're not, are you? Listen boy, you just show me where your boat is, and I'll see to it that nobody gets hurt. Do we understand each other?"

He wasn't a treasure hunter, he was a pirate. And he was trying to scare me. And it was working, but I couldn't let him know that. I just had to get free of his grip, then I could run. He would never catch me; he was too heavy, and too old.

"Okay, okay. I'll show you."

"Of course you will. And I'll show *you* something, just in case you get to thinking you might take a little run and forget all about me." He pulled a knife from his jacket. "See that coffee sign on the side of that shack?"

"Yah."

"See the picture of the girl?"

"Yah."

He raised his arm and flung the knife. It flew straight to the sign and struck the girl in the face. He had amazing aim. He pulled me over to the shack and dug the knife out. Then, he let me go. "Show me your boat."

I started walking towards the water, and he followed me. I kept thinking, maybe I could run for it. But I also kept imagining the knife sticking into my back. The water was so close, just a run and a jump. But I'd be an easy target for his knife. I had to do *something*; I couldn't lead him to the sub. Would I survive a knife wound? Not if it hit me in the head. And what if it struck me in the spine? It would cripple me. Then he'd probably just kill me anyway. There were no police here. I hadn't seen a single person on the street. No witnesses. No-body would ever know what had happened to me. I thought of Hollie waiting in the sub. If the man got into the sub, he'd kill him too. He didn't look like the sort of man who would care much for a little dog. Seaweed would survive. He was up in the sky somewhere. Seagulls can survive anywhere.

My chance to escape came at the very end of the street. I was almost close enough to jump. Just a couple of steps and I'd be clear. But was it a safe jump? I couldn't remember if there were rocks at the bottom. I couldn't jump if there were rocks. I tried to peer over the edge of the bluff as we approached the stairs that led down to the pier. My heart was beating fast. It had to be a split-second decision whether or not to jump. I had to catch him by surprise, before he could throw the knife. What should I do? Jump? Not jump? What were my other options? I tried to think. There weren't any. I reached the top of the stairs, took a glance over the edge, took one step, and flung myself off.

Air rushed into my face as I went down. The jump lasted only a couple of seconds, but it felt longer. I tensed my whole body to prepare for impact, and half expected to feel the knife stab me on the way down. It never did. But I never had a chance to jump with proper form, and hitting the water was almost like hitting the ground, except that it swallowed me up instead of flattening me out. Before I hit, I tried to grab a breath of air. I didn't want to come right back up where he could see me. I was hoping to swim under water to the sub, climb in, and motor away before he knew where I was.

But hitting the water knocked the wind out of me, and I couldn't do it. It was too far. I wasn't sure of the direction, either, and had to surface to look. I broke the surface as gently as possible, and gasped for air. Maybe he wouldn't see me if I just stuck my face above the water. No, he saw me. He was coming down the stairs towards the pier. He was going to reach it before me. I took a breath, and went under again.

Maybe I could trick him into thinking I was swimming down shore. I swam twenty feet or so, and surfaced. I waited until he saw me, then took another breath, and did it again. He must have thought I was swimming away, but he hadn't left the pier yet. The next time I went under, I went right to the bottom and doubled back towards the pier. It was twenty-five feet deep. He couldn't spot me. But this time I had to go all the way to the pier without surfacing.

It was so far. My lungs were bursting by the time I reached the sub. I went under it and up the other side. I broke the surface and sucked air into my lungs as quietly as I could. Had he fallen for the trick and gone down the shore, or was he right above my head? I reached for the handle on the side of the sub and started to climb up. But the water that dripped from me made a small noise. There was a heavy shuffling of feet above me and a scraping sound. As I climbed onto the portal and reached for the wheel to spin open the hatch, I saw him drop his head over the edge of the pier and look down at me. "You! You! . . ." He was furious. I spun open the hatch, climbed in, and shut it. I jumped down inside, rushed to the control panel, hit the dive and battery switches, put the sub in gear, and steered out from under the pier. As we came out, we started down. We couldn't dive more than fifteen feet, but at least we could get out of sight.

As we cleared the posts of the pier, I felt a heavy weight land on the hull. He had jumped onto the sub! He was insane! What did he think he could do? Would he try to open the hatch? But we were already under the surface. If he opened it now, the sub would flood and sink. Hollie would drown.

I had to pull us out of the dive because it was so shallow. We were going to hit bottom. We would hit hard, too, if we didn't slow down. I had to shut off the power. We would still hit, but maybe it wouldn't be so bad. It was a sandy bottom. It probably wouldn't damage the sub. And then, I heard the wheel spin on the hatch. He was opening it! He was trying to sink us!

I raced up the ladder and grabbed the hatch just as water started to spray inside. With my feet against the sides, I hung upside down and pulled down with all my might as he pulled up. He was so strong! The hatch opened an inch, and water poured in. I held on with all that I had. He was holding his breath under water. How long could he keep doing that?

He was too strong for me. The hatch opened two inches, and water flooded in. We were going to sink. And then, finally, the sub struck bottom and the jolt knocked him off his grip and I pulled the hatch shut. I spun it quickly, sealed it, then waited to see if he would turn it again. He didn't. He had gone to the surface for air. I jumped back inside, let enough air inside the tanks to rise off the bottom, engaged the batteries, and headed out to sea.

There was a foot of water on the floor, but the sump pumps were running and would clear the water in a few minutes. Hollie had jumped onto my hanging cot, where it was dry. He was chewing on a piece of rope as if nothing had happened. He had seen water flood into the sub before. Seaweed was still out, up in the sky somewhere, so we couldn't leave yet.

A quarter of a mile out, I shut off the power, raised the periscope, and looked back. The crazy pirate had swum to shore. I saw him stagger out of the water. I surfaced, climbed the portal, opened the hatch, and took a closer look with binoculars. He went straight to an orange, rubberized dinghy with a small outboard motor. He pushed it into the water, pulled the motor's cord, sat down, and sped off towards the small sailboat sitting a couple of hundred feet from the pier. It took him only a few minutes. He tied the dinghy to the boat, pulled up anchor and went inside the cabin. I scanned the stern of the boat for a name. *Maggie's Delight*. There were flowers painted around the name and on the sides of the boat. That wasn't his boat. There was no way that was his boat. He must have stolen it. I wondered what had happened to the crew. Did he kill them? He wasn't a treasure hunter at all; he was nothing but a pirate—greedy and cruel.

When he came out, he started bringing her around. Was he planning to chase us? That would be ridiculous. That would be like a turtle trying to catch a bat. And yet, he made me nervous. He was the nastiest person I had ever met. I bet he would rather die than give up chasing somebody. I sure hoped we'd never run into him again.

But we couldn't leave until we had picked up our first mate. I shut the hatch, submerged, sat down at the control panel, and turned on the sonar screen. There he was in the sailboat, coming towards us. He was dreaming if he thought he could catch us. I engaged the batteries and sailed in an arc around him, so that by the time he reached where we had been, we were back in the bay where we had started. I raised the periscope and watched him sail away, searching for us. When the little sailboat disappeared around the point, I surfaced, opened the hatch, and waited for my first mate to return. Finally he dropped out of the sky with a noisy flapping of his wings. Instead of jumping inside and looking for something to eat right away, as he would normally do, he paused on the hatch for a moment, and stared at me as if I were a stranger. "What? . . . Oh yah." I reached up and felt my head. "It's me, Seaweed. I just had a haircut." He twisted his head and stared at me as if I were from another planet. "I got skinned. So what?"

At least I didn't have a knife in my back.

# Chapter Three

THE INDIAN OCEAN flows gently and warmly down the southeast coast of Africa. It's a sleepy part of the world. The grass and palm trees are yellow and green, and the earth is brown and red. There are no mountains close to the water, but there are lots of beaches and lagoons and swampy areas along the shore. The coast is unbelievably shallow, the shallowest I have ever seen. In some places the drop-off is so far from the beach, you can walk out a mile in water up to your knees. Where we couldn't bring the sub close to shore—when we wanted to get out and walk on the beach—I'd inflate the rubber kayak and we'd paddle in. Then Hollie would run around on the sand, collect sticks and bits of rope, and chase crabs into the water. But sometimes the crabs would raise their claws and stare him down. Then Seaweed would attack them and eat them. I don't think those crabs had ever seen such a ferocious seagull before.

I always searched for secluded beaches. It wasn't that I didn't like meeting people. I did. I just worried that they might report us to local authorities when they saw the submarine, although I hadn't seen a single coastguard ship or police boat. There must have been some somewhere; I just hadn't seen them.

The people on shore were very poor, even poorer than in India. Sometimes I would sail close enough to watch them with the binoculars. Most lived in thatched bamboo huts. I saw old people sitting on the sand, staring at the water. I saw kids kicking soccer balls. The men fished in open boats they hauled up on the sand by hand, just as they did in India. But here, the boats were smaller; not much bigger than canoes. There were resorts here, too, for rich people and tourists, as in India, but fewer of them. And they were smaller, and not as fancy.

I kept a lookout for *Maggie's Delight*, but for three days never caught sight of her, although we were sailing as slowly as a sea turtle and spending more time on the beach than in the sub. I kept the hatch open the whole time, and Seaweed climbed in and out like a cat changing his mind. He flew quite a bit in the daytime, soaring above us like a kite. At night, he sat on the hull, keeping an eye open for trouble. Hollie created a salty pile of the loose bits of rope and sticks he had collected from the beach, and slowly chewed them into a frothy mulch. He liked the salty taste. The days were hot and muggy; the nights were warm and filled with stars. You would have thought we were sailing on a magical sea.

Then, on the fourth day, I detected a vessel on radar about fifteen miles offshore. We were approaching Mozambique Island, a tiny island with an old Portuguese port from the days of tall ships, just like Fort Kochi in India, across the sea. But Mozambique Island had an imposing fortress, with cannons still pointing at passing ships. It was also connected to the mainland by a narrow bridge. I had read about it in my guidebook, and it sounded really cool. I wanted to see it. I just hoped I wouldn't see that pirate there.

The vessel on radar was sailing slowly, like a sailboat. And then, it stopped. That made me curious. I wanted to check it out anyway, just to make sure it wasn't *Maggie's Delight*, so I followed it. Raising the periscope a quarter of a mile away, I spotted the flowery hull. It was her all right. She had the orange dinghy in tow. It didn't look like the pirate was intending to sail into Mozambique Island, being so far offshore at this point. But why had he stopped? Then, I saw why, though I could hardly believe it.

He climbed the mast with a rope. The little boat tossed side to side with his weight. He reached up and tied the rope as close to the top of the mast as he could, and shimmied down. Then, he climbed into the dinghy, tied down the other end of the rope, pulled the engine cord, motored to the port side . . . then sped away! As the dinghy motored away, it pulled the mast of the sailboat down and swamped the boat. He was sinking her! She was too slow for him, and he was hiding the evidence of his theft.

Once the boat was down, he untied the rope, coiled it up in the dinghy, and sped off towards Mozambique Island.

I waited until he was out of sight, surfaced, and motored over to the boat. She hadn't sunk yet. But she had rolled completely around, and her mast was pointing to the bottom. I always found it sad when a boat sank. I didn't know why; it wasn't a person. It still felt like a death to me.

I opened the hatch, climbed out of the portal and, grabbing a handle on the side of the sub, I reached over with my foot and touched the hull of the sailboat. She would sink soon. I didn't really want to see that, so I stood up and turned around. And then, I heard it. At least I thought I heard it. I wasn't sure. Maybe it was just my imagination, but I could have sworn I heard a weak voice say "Maggie." It was very faint. I stood still, closed my eyes, and listened carefully. There was a little wind, but no sound from the water. No, I didn't hear anything. It was just my imagination. It bugged me, though. I reached over and tapped the hull again. Maybe one push was all it would take to send her to the bottom. I turned around, and then I heard it again. "Maggie." Good Lord! There was someone inside the boat!

I had to act fast; the boat was going to sink. But if someone was inside, why didn't they climb out? Were they locked inside? Were they tied up? How horrible! Would that pirate do such a thing? I guess he would. "Act!" I said to myself.

I jumped into the water, beat against the side of the boat with my fist and yelled, "I'm coming to help you!" Then I took a breath, and went under.

I found the base of the mast where the keel should have been. The door to the cabin was behind it, near the stern. I swam over and pulled on the door. It was locked! It would take a screwdriver to pry it open. I had to return to the sub.

If I were going inside the boat, I would have to go on a rope. Then, if it started to sink, I could pull myself out, so long as the rope didn't get hung up. It would be dark inside, so I'd have to carry a flashlight. I'd also need both hands free. I stripped down to my shorts. I didn't want any clothing to get caught on a hook or nail. I cut a piece of twine, tied it to the hook on the bottom of the flashlight, and hung it around my neck. Then I grabbed a long screwdriver. I took a fifty-foot coil of rope, climbed the portal, tied one end of the rope to the harness, and the other end to a handle on the hull of the sub, strapped the harness on, climbed out, and shut the hatch.

I jumped into the water, took a breath, and went under again. There were windows in the cabin, but they were underwater. I couldn't see inside them. I found the door, shoved the screwdriver into the jamb, and pulled as hard as I could.

If the door opened, it was going to let a whole lot of water into the boat in a hurry. I would have to find whoever was inside, and get them out. But what if they were tied up? Or what if they were injured? What if I couldn't save them?

The door gave a little. Bubbles blew into my face. I kept at it, but was using up my air. I had to surface again. The boat had sunk deeper. It was going to plunge to the bottom any moment. I took a breath and went under again, found the door, jammed the screwdriver in, and pulled with all my might. The door burst open. Air rushed out and water rushed in. I clicked on the flashlight and swung it around the cabin. There was nobody here! And it was filling with water. I had to get out. I looked one last time. No, there was no one here. Strange, I was so sure I had heard someone. It must have been my imagination. I took a breath of the cabin air and got ready to leave. Then, I heard the voice coming from a small compartment in the bow. "Maggie!"

There was someone locked inside a very small space. "I'm coming!" I yelled. "I will help you!"

"Maggie!" came the voice again. But it was very weak. And it was strange. It almost sounded like a recording.

"Hold on! I'm coming!"

I moved towards the door, but the rope went taut and held me back. The boat was sinking now. No! I pulled hard, but the rope wouldn't budge. Then, it pulled me back a few feet. The cabin was more than half full of water. The boat was going down.

"Open the door!" I yelled. "I can't reach!"

There was no answer, and no sound from inside the compartment. Maybe it was filling with water, too.

"Open the door!"

No one answered. I tried with all my might to reach, but the rope just kept pulling me back. We were both going to drown if we didn't get out now.

"Maggie!"

The rope pulled me back even further. There was no fighting it. I had to take the harness off. I knew I shouldn't do that, but what choice did I have? Could I sail away from this boat knowing someone had drowned, but that maybe I could have saved them? Would I be able to live with that? No. I thought of Hollie and Seaweed. I was risking their lives, too, if I didn't make it back. But what else could I do?

I unbuckled the harness and felt it slip away. The cabin was two-thirds full, and the boat was tilting. It was sinking. I rushed at the door, shoved the screwdriver into the jamb, and twisted it open. There was no one there! "Maggie!" came the voice again, louder this time. I stuck my head inside the compartment and finally saw who it was.

It was a bird in a cage. The cage was upside-down and the bird was clinging to the bars. It looked like a small parrot. The cage was attached to a hook. Water was flooding the compartment. How could I get the bird out without drowning it?

I dropped the screwdriver, grabbed the cage, and pulled it free from the hook. There was a vinyl tablecloth floating on the water. I picked it up and wrapped it around the cage, held the cage above water, and started back through the cabin. The boat was almost vertical now. I took a deep breath and peeked into the cage. The bird stared back at me, and I had the strangest thought that it knew what we were about to do. "Good luck!" I said. I had such a bad feeling inside. I didn't think it was going to make it. I pulled the tablecloth tight, gripped it hard with one hand, took another breath, and went under the water and out of the boat.

It didn't surprise me that we were already ten feet under-water. I kicked off the hull of the boat. It took just a few seconds to reach the surface. The cage was pulling me up, too, so it must have trapped some air. I sure hoped the bird would survive.

When we broke the surface, I lifted the cage up. Water poured out of it. I grabbed the side of the sub and climbed up. When I pulled the tablecloth off the cage, the bird lifted its head and looked at me. It was soaking wet. "You're lucky," I said. It shook out its feathers and opened its beak as if it were trying to spit up water. It stared at me with shiny eyes. Then it squawked. "Rough seas! Rough seas!"

# Chapter Four

THE CREW WASN'T pleased when I brought the little bird inside. Seaweed scowled, and Hollie whined. They might have been even less pleased had they known she was a girl. Her name was painted in bright pink and yellow letters on the front of her cage. *Little Laura*. I wondered what had happened to big Laura, or to Maggie. Were they still alive? I wished I could tell them that Little Laura had escaped from that pirate. He had doomed her to a watery grave. But, like Hollie, who had been thrown into the sea with a rope around his neck when he was a puppy, she was destined to live.

I carried the cage inside and looked around for a place to

hang it. There was a little metal dish inside, and a swing; nothing else. I bet she hadn't been fed for a long time. "I'll hang your cage from the ceiling. We'd better find you some food."

I knew that parrots liked fruit, seeds, and nuts, so I grabbed a handful of peanuts and raisins, opened the cage door gently, and dropped them inside. I lifted out the metal dish, filled it with water, and put it back. Boy, was that bird hungry and thirsty! For half an hour I watched it go back and forth between the food and water. Hollie wouldn't stop whining, so I picked him up, and let him watch, too. Back and forth Little Laura hopped, grinding peanuts with her beak and gobbling droplets of water. And she watched us watching her.

Meanwhile, *Maggie's Delight* settled on her side four hundred feet below. On sonar, I saw her stop falling, turn slowly on to her side, and lie still. There she would stay forever. It was dark at four hundred feet, but not as dark, I imagined, as the heart of the man who had put her there.

Little Laura was a challenge for Hollie and Seaweed. They didn't like her at first. I couldn't help wondering if it was because she was stubborn, like them. When I held Hollie close to the cage, which was what he wanted, Little Laura would come over to him with her beak open wide, and he would back away, afraid of getting bitten. Then he would look at me as if to say, does she have to be here? I wanted to open her door and give her the freedom to come out, but I was afraid that Seaweed would attack her. He looked at her as if she were a crab. I wasn't afraid of Hollie hurting her; he wanted to be friends with everyone. But Seaweed was a very aggressive seagull, and seemed to regard Little Laura as an intruder. So, I waited until he was outside before I opened the door.

As soon as the door was open, Little Laura climbed out and up on top of her cage. She looked all around the sub, then climbed down to the bottom of the cage, and hung upside down, and looked around. I wondered if she might try to fly, but she didn't. Then I wondered if she could fly. One of her wings seemed shorter than the other. She looked like she wanted to climb down, so I cut a piece of rope long enough to reach the floor, and tied it to the bottom of her cage. While I was tying it, she kept her beak open as if she would bite me. When I was done, she climbed halfway down the rope. She seemed to have her eye on Hollie's pile of ropes and sticks. He looked up at her nervously. I sat down on the floor to watch what would happen next.

Little Laura worked her way down the rope like an acrobat without much balance. When she was a few inches from the bottom, she stopped, hung upside down, and looked to see if the coast was clear. Then she stepped onto the floor and stood up. She was pretty small. Hollie got up, pretended to ignore her, picked up one of his sticks, and put it on his pile. Little Laura made a kind of cakewalk towards the pile. She reminded me of Charlie Chaplin. I watched Hollie to make sure he wouldn't suddenly turn aggressive against the little bird. He didn't. He just looked worried.

Little Laura eyed the pile of sticks and rope. But every time she got close to a piece of it, Hollie would get up and move it somewhere else. Still, the little bird wouldn't quit. Eventually, she closed her beak on the end of a small stick and dragged it back towards the rope. That wasn't easy, because the stick was too big for her. There was no way she could carry it up to her cage. But that didn't stop her from trying. Once she pulled it to the bottom of the rope, Hollie got up, walked over quietly, picked up the stick, and carried it back. Little Laura opened her beak wide and lunged at him, but he just ignored her. Then, she started the whole thing over again. I got tired of watching, so I got up and made some tea.

I was sitting on my cot, drinking my tea, and eating an orange, when Seaweed dropped down the portal. He came in like a chimney sweep, with a noisy rustling of his feathers. I jumped to my feet because I knew Little Laura was on the floor. Seaweed liked to come in, check for food, plop down on his spot by the observation window, and be left alone while he slept.

There was no food in sight, so Seaweed went straight for his spot. But Little Laura stood in his way. It looked like David standing in front of Goliath. I followed Seaweed over and stayed ready to rescue the little bird. Little Laura had her beak open. Seaweed wasn't impressed with that. He opened his beak and lunged at her as if he were going to swallow her up.

"No! Seaweed! Don't!" But before I could grab him, Little Laura lunged back at him, and Seaweed stopped. He leaned forward with his beak wide open, trying to intimidate the little bird. But she reached up and tried to intimidate him right back. I think that impressed him. It was a stand-off. To change the mood, I gave each bird a piece of my orange. That ended the conflict. Seaweed gobbled his in an instant and looked for more. Little Laura picked up hers and began the long climb up the rope to her cage. It was a lot of work. Half way up, the piece of orange slipped from her beak, fell to the floor, and Seaweed gobbled it up. Little Laura hung upside down and just stared. I felt sorry for her then so I peeled another orange and put a couple of pieces in her cage. What a tough little bird.

But she was afraid of me. She would always open her beak when my fingers were near, or when I'd put fresh water or food in her cage. I'd reach out my hand and say, "Come!" But she never would. And yet I thought she was lonely. She seemed to want Hollie's company the most. But he didn't want to have anything to do with her. She would climb all the way down the rope and approach him. She wouldn't try to take his ropes or sticks anymore; she would just pick at them. But it looked like what she really wanted was his attention. She even approached his tail once, but he didn't like that, got up and turned around. Then he plopped down, stared at her, and sighed. But she wouldn't give up.

I started leaving her cage door open when I went to bed

because she liked to go in and out so much, and I didn't want her to feel locked in. But once, when I got up for a drink of water, I couldn't find her. I looked at Seaweed. He was as still as a stone. I looked at Hollie. He was curled up, watching me, but not moving. Where was Little Laura? She wasn't in her cage. I started looking around on the floor. Maybe she had crawled into a small space to hide. Nope, she wasn't anywhere. I started to worry. I stared at the crew again. Seaweed hadn't so much as blinked, but it seemed to me that Hollie was looking a little suspicious. I stepped closer. Now, he looked downright guilty. "Hollie. Do you know where . . . ?" And then, I saw her. She was lying on her belly, tucked in against Hollie's side. I looked closely to make sure she was still alive. Yup. Her little belly was rising and falling. Hollie looked at me as if to say, it isn't my fault. What else was I supposed to do?

"You're a good dog, Hollie."

After that, Hollie and Little Laura became friends. I kind of wondered if they shared a special bond in that, both having come so close to death, they knew that other creatures were quite willing to kill them. I wondered if they recognized that feeling in each other.

# Chapter Five

I SHOULD HAVE SAILED away from Mozambique Island altogether. I knew that. And I wished I could have. It was surely the most dangerous place for me to be right now. But I remembered something my grandfather had once told me—that if you knew someone was going to do something wrong and you didn't try to stop them, then you became responsible, too. I knew why that pirate had gone to the island. He was hoping to steal a faster boat. And maybe he would kill someone to get it. Was he really that ruthless? Judging from what I had seen so far, I believed he was. What if it were a family? What if there were children? My guidebook said there were

twelve thousand people on the island. It also had a police station. Maybe if I could find it, and tell them everything I had
witnessed, they would bring him in and question him. Then,
once they saw what he was like, they might believe me. Maybe they wouldn't put him behind bars, where he belonged,
but would at least keep an eye on him. I sure as heck didn't
want to run into him again, but didn't see how I could avoid
going to the island to warn them. It seemed to me this was
one of those times my grandfather had been talking about.

The island was barely approachable by sub, unless we sailed
on the surface, which we couldn't do in the daytime. I would
have liked to sail completely around it, and see where the
orange dinghy was moored, but the water was simply too
shallow. I scouted as much as I could from a distance through
the periscope in the late afternoon. There was a long bridge
that spanned the channel between the mainland and island
on the western side, but we couldn't get close to it.

By twilight, we were sitting just north of the island, where
the fort was. I brought the sub to a hundred feet from the
fort's stone wall, surfaced so that the portal was showing only
six inches above water, opened the hatch, and tossed the anchor. There was little current, and there were stones sticking
out of the water that helped disguise us. Once it was dark, I
inflated the kayak, shut the hatch, and went for a paddle. No
one would see me as long as I stayed in the dark. The lighted
areas were in the middle and south of the island, where the
people were. The north was shrouded in darkness.

I paddled all the way down the ocean side, around the bottom, up the mainland side, and under the bridge. I didn't see a single pier. Boats were either moored at anchor, or hauled up on the beach. Tucked in between fishing boats on the sand, I found the orange dinghy.

Don't be nervous, I told myself, just be careful. Find the police station, and tell them what you know. But what could I tell them—that a man had grabbed me, sank a boat that probably belonged to somebody else, and almost killed a bird? What if they didn't believe me? What proof did I have? None. Still, I knew in my heart that he had come here to steal someone else's boat, and I didn't think he would hesitate to kill somebody to get it.

I paddled a little closer and looked carefully at the beach. There was no one on the sand, but there were lights beneath the palm trees and between small houses. The houses were made of stone and wood and had thatched roofs. I could hear music playing and voices laughing. It sounded like cafés.

I stared at the dinghy. I felt an urge to just run up on the beach, puncture its skin with my jackknife, and run back. Then, the air would leak out, and he couldn't motor out and steal someone's boat. At least it would slow him down. I reached into my pocket. Rats! I wasn't carrying my knife. There must be something else I could do?

I paddled to the beach, climbed out, and crept up to the dinghy with my head down. My heart was beating fast. If I had more time, I might try to open the casing of the outboard motor and pull out some wires. Instead, I unscrewed the gas tank, reached down, grabbed handfuls of sand, and poured them into the tank. I moved as quickly as I could, and kept looking up the beach to see if anyone was coming. I poured *a lot* of sand into that tank. The engine might start, but it sure wouldn't go far. The pirate was going to be furious. At least now he would know that somebody was watching him, and knew what he was up to.

I put the cap back on, turned to go, and froze. There was a little old man sitting on the sand in the dark not more than fifteen feet away from me. He had been watching me the whole time. He looked as though he had been hired to watch the dinghy, yet he never did anything. I looked at him to see if he was going to yell out, but he just stared as if he were staring right through me, as if he didn't even see me. I figured he didn't want to see me. He didn't want to get caught in the middle of trouble. And he must have known there was trouble coming.

I ran back to the kayak, jumped in, and paddled away. I paddled all the way around the island and back to the fort. Along the way, I saw a sailboat motoring towards the south of the island from the open sea. It was hard to see in the dark, but I thought I saw the silhouettes of several people on deck. There were no lights on the boat, which was strange, though I didn't give it much thought at the time. I paddled back to a spot just beyond the sub, tied up the kayak, climbed the wall, and jumped into the fort.

I would have liked to walk around the fort, explore the dungeons, and climb the cannon, but I couldn't stop now. I had to find the police station. Maybe I could explore on my way back. I cut through the big courtyard, climbed over the front gate, and headed towards the centre of the island. I was hungry now. If Mozambique Island had 12,000 people, maybe it had pizza, too. Maybe I could find one after talking to the police.

I crossed a sandy soccer field and a treed park and found myself on a street with houses. There were people sitting outside as I went down the street. I smiled and waved at them, and they smiled and waved back. I had learned that people in other countries will always be friendly to you if you smile at them. Most of the people in the world are really friendly.

There were lots of houses, and a few stone buildings with shops and offices in them. Everything was old. All of the roofs on the houses were thatched, but the roofs of the buildings were made of clay shingles. It was a warm night, and the atmosphere in the town was relaxed and friendly. I heard music. Then, I saw a few cafés. I knew I had to watch out for the pirate now. But he would be easy to spot. He would stand out from these people like a rotten cabbage in a field of strawberries.

But I never saw him. I came upon a café where they were grilling fish out front, and the smell was so good, I thought I would die if I didn't eat some. There were chairs around a picnic table, and a waiter pulled one out and gestured for me to sit, so I did. Then, he brought me a plate of fish and a tall glass of fresh pineapple juice to wash it down. I don't think anything ever tasted as good as that meal. But all the time that I ate, I kept a lookout for a large man in the street.

As I was leaving the café, I asked the waiter if he could tell me where the police station was. A very friendly man, he suddenly looked concerned. He pointed quickly in one direction, then frowned and lowered his head. When I paid for my meal, I gave him a dollar for a tip. He shook my hand, hugged my shoulder, and shook my hand again. He said something else about the police station, but I didn't understand. Then he lowered his head again, and shook it. I took that as a warning not to trust the police. It didn't entirely surprise me. In some countries you can trust the police; in others, you can't. Richer countries can afford to pay their police force. Poor countries sometimes can't, so the police officers have to make their money some other way, which isn't always legal. I thanked the friendly waiter and walked away.

Two streets west, I found the police station. It didn't look like much. It was just a small building with one light on. I was standing across the street, wondering whether I should listen to the waiter and leave, or take a chance and go in, when, suddenly, the door opened and out walked the pirate!

I didn't know if he saw me or not. I backed up into the darkness of the trees. He looked angry. He stormed down the street towards the beach. A policeman stood in the doorway of the station and watched him go. I waited until the policeman went back inside, then followed the pirate at a distance. He was too big and heavy to catch me at a run, and I noticed now that he had a bit of a limp. But I had to stay out of his knife-throwing range; that was for sure.

He went down a few more streets and turned into an alley that led to a café. The music was loud, and so were the people. Through the trees, I saw a few rougher types, like him. They were standing around with bottles in their hands, yelling and laughing and slapping each other's backs. He disappeared amongst them.

I was about to go back to the sub then, and leave, but there was one thing I wanted to know. Why had he gone to the police station? Was it possible he had tried the motor of his dinghy and discovered it had been sabotaged? Was that it? It was kind of hard to believe that a pirate would complain to the police though, unless the police were corrupt too, which was what the waiter had been suggesting. But the whole thing didn't make sense, and it made me so curious I thought I'd swing by the beach and just take another peek at the dinghy.

The old man was sitting in the same spot. I knew he saw me when I came over; I saw his head turn. He was just pretending not to see me. In the dark, I wasn't sure if the dinghy had been moved or not. I thought maybe it had. "Did a big man try to move this boat?" I asked the old man. He didn't answer. I reached into my pocket, found a dollar bill, and put it down on the sand in front of him. He picked up the dollar, looked up at me, and nodded. Then he got to his feet, pulled his thumb across his neck as a way of warning me to be careful, and disappeared in the dark. Now I knew. It was time to get out of here.

Just as I was about to leave the beach, I noticed the dark sailboat motoring down from the north of the island. It looked like a ghost on the water. They must have gone right around the island when they discovered the bridge in their way. I stepped closer to the water to try to see them more clearly. Then I heard heavy feet in the sand. I never had a chance.

# Chapter Six

THE FIRST BLOW STRUCK me on the head and knocked me down. I hit the ground at the edge of the water and got wet sand in my face. Before I had a chance to get up, he grabbed hold of me, pulled me halfway up, and hit me again. He struck me on the side of the head and I went flat against the sand. My ears were ringing and I was seeing black and red spots. He hit me really hard. Then he grabbed me, pulled me up, and I saw his knife flash through the air. He's going to stab me, I thought. I'm going to die.

"Pour sand into my motor will you, you little crook!"

Who was he calling a crook? I was so dizzy now I thought I'd faint. I hoped he didn't hit me again.

"You sank *Maggie's Delight*! What did you do with Maggie? Did you kill her?"

He pulled me around so he could look me in the eye. One side of my face was burning and swelling. "You know a lot more than you should, kid. You and me are gonna get better acquainted. The first thing you're gonna do is show me that little submarine you've got. Then maybe I won't cut your liver out, which is what I was going to do. Or maybe you think I won't do that, do you?"

I knew he would. I knew he would do anything. Now I felt certain he had killed Maggie, and probably other people, too. I also knew I had to escape from him, somehow, somewhere between here and the sub. He had been drinking. I could smell it on him. Perhaps he would trip and fall. Perhaps I could push him or trip him—anything just so I could run. He couldn't throw the knife at me in the dark. He probably couldn't throw straight when he was drunk, either. For now, I just had to go along with him.

"I'll take you to the sub. It's at the north of the island, outside the wall."

"Kid, if it's not where you say it is, you're gonna hurt really bad. You understand me?"

"I understand. It's there. I'll show you."

We started walking. This time, he didn't let go of me. He held my wrist, and his hand felt like a vise. I could feel my hand losing blood. "You're holding my wrist too tight."

"You're lucky you still have a hand. I should've cut it off.

You put . . ." He stopped. Three men appeared in front of us in the dark. He spun around quickly, pulling me with him. There were three men behind us, too. We were surrounded. They were young men. They reminded me of the Somali pirates I had seen on TV. I saw light reflect off something in one of the men's hands. It was a knife.

"Did you think we wouldn't fin' you, boss?" said one of the men. "You thought you 'ad lost us forever did you? Thought y'd never see us again, hey?"

"Boys . . . don't think I was cutting you out . . ."

"Where is it, Jonnyboy?" said another man. "We know you got it wit' you."

"Boys . . . did you think I would bring it here? You've got to be crazy . . ."

The men kept closing in, like a pack of dogs. My heart was beating fast. Were they going to attack me, too? Probably. I was waiting for a chance to break free and run, but his grip on my wrist only got tighter. I glanced up the beach towards the trees and chose which way I would run. Would they chase me? Would they catch me? They weren't as big as him, but there were six of them. If I could just get free of his grip, I would run as fast as I could.

He spun me around again, to face the men in front of us. Now, I saw two more blades. He saw them, too. I felt him reach for his knife with his other hand. This was my chance. I had to take it now; I might not get another. I raised my foot and kicked down on the side of his knee as hard as I could. It caught him off-guard, as I hoped, then I smashed my other fist against his hand, pulled my hand free, and ran up the beach with everything I had in me. I heard yelling and scuffling behind me. They were attacking him now, but I didn't stop, and never turned around. I ran off the sand, between the trees, and onto the first street I saw. I ran to the end of it, and down the next. I ran so fast I thought my lungs would burst. Near the end of the second street, I turned my head to see if anyone had chased me. No. Nobody had.

I stopped and bent over to catch my breath. I felt sick from running so hard, and from what had just happened. Those men had clearly come here to murder him. They had probably been following him for a long time. It sounded like he had cheated them. But they had caught up with him.

I felt conflicted. I wondered if I should have tried to help him, or if I should maybe even go back now and see if he was okay. But that was crazy. Even if I could have saved him, which I couldn't, wouldn't he just kill me anyway, once I had taken him to the sub? Would he treat me differently because I had helped him? I had no reason to think he would. He wanted my sub. It was the perfect vessel for a pirate. I'm sure he would have killed me for it, whether I had helped him or not. Still, it didn't feel good running away from someone who was in trouble.

I walked and ran back to the sub, looking over my shoulder the whole way. There was mist in the air now, and scattered fog was drifting across the north of the island. It made me a little nervous as I retraced my steps through the fort. There were so many dark shadows. What if the other pirates had come this way after they had killed him? Or, what if he had escaped from them and was still looking for me, angrier than ever? Was it possible he had fought them off? No, I didn't think so. I didn't see how that was possible. But what if he had, and was hiding in the shadows right now, waiting to catch me and cut out my liver?

More likely, he was lying on the sand, bleeding to death, or was already dead.

The fog covered the rocks and the portal of the sub. But I knew where the kayak was, and was able to find the sub by paddling straight out from the wall. I climbed onto the portal, opened the hatch, jumped in, and greeted my crew. They were happy to see me, but not as happy as I was to see them. What if I hadn't returned? I hated to think of what would have happened to them. After I deflated the kayak and packed it away, I fed the crew, put the kettle on for tea, sat on my cot, and considered what to do.

Part of me wanted to head out to sea and sail away. Part of me wanted to see if I could spot the pirates from the water. But it was dark and unlikely that I'd see them. And another part of me wanted to go to the police and tell them everything that had happened. Had it been anywhere else, I believe I would have done that, but I didn't trust the police here, or think it was safe for me to tell them what I knew.

So, I decided to sail away. I surfaced and turned on the

engine. No one would see us in the dark, especially in the fog. I climbed the portal to take one last look at the north of the island before leaving. Only patches were visible, but the moment my eyes fell on it, I felt a nagging in my conscience. I didn't really want to admit it, but something was bothering me. What if the pirate who had beaten me and threatened to kill me, what if he was lying on the beach, wounded, but still alive? What if he was bleeding to death but would survive if he could make it to a hospital? Could I sail away thinking maybe I had let him die, even a terrible man like him? Or would it haunt me for the rest of my life?

I felt the side of my face. It was bruised and swollen and very sore. If those men hadn't come for him, he would surely have killed me. And then he would have killed Hollie and Seaweed, and Little Laura, and stolen the sub. So why should I go back and check on him? I didn't know, but the very fact that I had to ask myself that question told me it would haunt me. I had to return so that I could know I had done the right thing. It was enough that he had attacked me. I didn't want him to haunt me, too.

So I shut off the kettle and sailed down the mainland side of the island slowly and cautiously. It was shallow, but that was not a problem as long as I didn't try to submerge. At the first sign of trouble, I would simply turn around, crank up the engine, and take off.

It was hard to see the beach clearly in the darkness and fog. I tried to identify the spot where I had run through the trees, but too many places looked the same. I went down until I was sure we had passed the spot, turned around, and started back up. Maybe he had gotten to his feet and walked away, or maybe they had carried him, or . . . I hated to think of it . . . buried him already. If I didn't see a body on the beach, I would sail away. I wasn't going to search the whole island for him.

After a while, I thought maybe we were next to the beach where the fight took place, but I wasn't sure. There was no body on the sand, at least none that I could see. I stopped the sub, stood up on the hatch with the binoculars, and stared through the mist. No, there was nothing there. Maybe he had survived, after all. Maybe they had stopped fighting, or he had taken them to whatever it was they were looking for— money probably, or the treasure he had talked about. But no, there was nobody here. I started the engine again, and continued.

Just a little further north, where the sand gave way to a rocky area, I thought I saw a dark shape on the ground. I stood up on the hatch again, and looked. Yup, looked like a body to me. I shut the engine, inflated the kayak, closed the hatch behind me, and paddled to the beach. I looked carefully to make sure there was no one else around. The closer I got to the dark shape, the more certain I felt it was him. When I climbed out of the kayak and pulled it up onto the beach, I knew for sure. He was lying face down on the rocks, not moving at all. I had seen dead bodies before. There's something different in the look of a dead body, even in the dark. It's hard to explain, but once a person is dead, their body is no different from the body of a dead cow, or even a dead tree. It is no longer a person. It becomes something else.

Even though I was certain he was dead, I approached carefully. What if he were playing dead? What if he were wounded, but still alive, just waiting for me to get close enough that he could stab me?

I stepped closer, reached over, and poked him with the paddle. It was like poking a heavy bag of sand. He was definitely dead. I came closer still, bent down, and pulled him over. He was so heavy! I figured I'd better check his pulse. I didn't want to, but thought I should. His hands were large, and scarred, like his face. I put my fingers on his wrist, where the pulse ought to be. There was no warmth there, the way there should be in a living body. I couldn't find a pulse. I moved my fingers several times looking for one. I pressed harder. No, there was nothing there.

I stood up and stared at him. He had been stabbed many times. I could see the tears in his clothing and the darkness of blood. There was blood on his neck and chin. He had such a frightening face. He had been such a frightening man. But a strange feeling came over me, I didn't know why. I suddenly imagined him as he might have been when he was just a little boy—because there had been a time, a long time ago, when he had been a boy, just like any other boy. Here, now, he was lying dead on a beach, murdered. How sad it was, that a little boy, *any* boy, would ever end up like this. Who even knew all he had done in his life? How many crimes had he committed? Had he ever done anything good? Had he ever loved anyone? Surely somebody must have loved him, once upon a time? As I stood and stared at him, I started to feel terribly sad for him. I could barely hold back my tears.

But I did.

# Chapter Seven

SHOULD I WALK TO the police station to report the murder, and tell the policeman there everything I had witnessed? But what if he told me to stay around to testify, and what if I couldn't leave for a long time? What if he didn't believe me, and kept me under suspicion? After all, I hadn't entered the country legally. I had never shown anyone my passport. Maybe he would put me behind bars until he sorted it all out. What would happen to my crew then? No, there was no way I could risk telling the police. I had been warned not to trust them. For a moment, I wondered if I ought to pull the body into the water, tow it a few miles out, and give it a burial at sea. But then I would be destroying the evidence of the crime, which would be helping the murderers, and creating another crime. And what if I got caught with the body? Everyone would believe I had killed him. No, I couldn't do that. I didn't see how I could do anything but leave. I would have to let somebody else find the body. But then, what if it were found by young kids playing on the beach? As I stood over the body and tried to figure it out, I caught a glimpse of a small mast in the fog. The dark sailboat!

That settled everything. I ran to the kayak, pushed it into the water, and raced to the sub. As I climbed up and opened the hatch, I saw the sailboat approaching slowly through the fog. Maybe they were coming to collect the body and hide what they had done.

There was no time to deflate the kayak. I tied it to the hatch, jumped inside, started the engine, and cranked it up. As we motored away, I looked back with the binoculars, but couldn't tell if they were stopping or not. Probably they were. I sailed around to the sea side of the island and half a mile out from shore. I deflated the kayak, folded it, and put it away. Then I put the kettle on again, sat at the radar screen, and waited for them to show.

I drank a cup of chamomile tea, with honey, but couldn't seem to settle down. My crew knew when I was upset or excited. They could feel the difference in my mood. And if I was calm and relaxed, or nervous and agitated, they reflected that. Seaweed stayed on his feet, ready to climb up the portal and jump into the air. Hollie picked up his ears, listened extra carefully to every sound, and sniffed the air. But not Little Laura. She cakewalked around the floor like a tiny penguin, picking up tiny bits of rope and wood that Hollie had dropped, and carrying them all the way up to her cage. She reminded me of Jack in the Beanstalk. It was so much work for her. Finally, it occurred to me to tie her cage closer to the floor. So I did. I hung it from a rope just two feet off the floor. She watched me do it, trying to bite me the whole time. But now, her climb was a lot shorter, and she went up and down a lot more often.

Half an hour later, there was a beep on the radar. A vessel appeared at the northern corner of the island. They were coming now.

I submerged, raised the periscope, and waited. Without lights, they were hard to spot. Sometimes they appeared as a dark shadow on the water, and sometimes they seemed to disappear. The closer they came, the better I could see them. The further from shore we were, the less fog there was. A mile out, there was none.

They came within a quarter of a mile of us, and I was starting to wonder if they had located us with a portable sonar device. But they hadn't. They came past and kept going, never knowing we were there. I engaged battery power and followed them. They were towing the orange dinghy.

They motored out three miles, and stopped. I surfaced a quarter of a mile away, climbed the portal, and watched them through the binoculars. They lit two lanterns and hung them from the mast. There were six pirates in the boat.

The first thing they did was climb into the dinghy, reach down and lift something heavy out, and drop it into the sea. I was certain it was the body, even though I couldn't see it clearly. Then, they started searching the dinghy. They were looking for something, but couldn't find it. They argued. I saw one man push another into the water. Eventually, they all climbed back onto the sailboat and went inside the cabin. I waited. A little while later, they came charging out of the cabin as if they had discovered something. They pulled the dinghy right out of the water and turned it upside down. They shone a flashlight on it. There was something attached to the bottom. It looked like a black garbage bag. I saw them get excited when they pulled it free. One man held it up in the air and I heard them cheer from quarter of a mile away.

The pirates headed back towards Mozambique Island. They must have thought they were safe now that they had destroyed the evidence of their crime. They turned off their lamps, motored around the north of the island, and back down the mainland side in the fog. I followed them. I couldn't help it. I just couldn't let them get away with it. It wasn't right. I didn't know what I could do, but I couldn't leave without doing something.

I had to surface to round the island again, but kept our distance. Through the binoculars, I watched them drop anchor down by the bridge. Five of them climbed into the dinghy and paddled to the beach, leaving one pirate behind to keep watch. I heard them laugh and shout. But the man on the boat was shouting with frustration and anger. He wasn't happy being left behind. I motored a little closer to see him better. He was carrying a small machine gun over his shoulder, the kind I've seen harbour police use in other countries. He was standing on the stern of the boat, watching his companions leave, no doubt to go to the café to celebrate having found whatever it was they had found.

I watched for half an hour. I could tell by his movements that the man on the boat was unhappy. He was hitting and kicking things. Finally, one of the other pirates yelled to him from the beach. I swung the binoculars over and saw him wave his arm. There was another man there, a small old man. I wondered if it was the man who had kept watch over the dinghy. It sure looked like him. The pirate on the boat put down his gun, jumped into the water, and swam to the beach. He greeted his companion happily, and they disappeared in the dark. The old man sat down on the sand and stared at the boat. I was sure it was him. This was my chance.

I wanted to get onto their boat and have a look. What was it they had taken from the man they had killed? Money? Treasure? I wanted to know. Maybe I could find it and take it. And then I could sabotage their boat so that they couldn't follow me. They were probably planning to spend hours at the café, drinking and celebrating. I would have time.

Switching to battery power, I snuck up behind their boat

from the mainland side, so that the old man wouldn't see or hear the sub. I doubted he could spot it in the dark anyway. I climbed out onto the hull, then jumped onto the bow of the sailboat. My heart was racing. The sailboat stank like rotten cheese. I crouched down and crept along the deck until I reached the door to the cabin. Not surprisingly, it was locked. So, I went back to the sub and grabbed a small crowbar and a flashlight. I took a peek through the binoculars to make sure the old man was still sitting on the beach. He was. I jumped back onto the sailboat.

The cabin door made some noise but gave way easily with the crowbar. I took a few steps down into the cabin, held the flashlight against my middle to make only a small light, turned it on, and took a look around.

I couldn't believe what I saw. The cabin was filled with guns, of every size. They were leaning against the walls and lying on the floor. There were handguns and machine guns and rifles. On a counter, where the sink, stove and fridge were, there were bundles of money, bags of white powder, and the plastic bag they had found on the bottom of the dinghy. It had been opened, and I saw the glitter of gold and jewellery. I couldn't believe it.

It didn't take me long to decide what to do. I would sabotage the boat, but not here. I went back to the sub and grabbed a hacksaw. I sawed through the anchor line, then tied a towing line from the portal of the sub to the bow of the sailboat. I took another glance at the old man sitting on the sand. He was as still as a wooden statue. I wondered if he was even awake. I wondered if he ever actually reported anything he saw. What would he think when he saw the sailboat sailing away by itself? I turned on the engine and cranked it up full blast. The sub's propeller churned up the water and the rope went taut. The bow of the sailboat spun around and came after us like a horse on a lead. As I towed the boat away, I took one last look at the old man, saw him rise to his feet, shake off the sand, and hurry off the beach.

# Chapter Eight

I TOWED THE SAILBOAT around the island and out to sea. It slowed us down quite a bit, and I knew it was only a matter of time before the pirates would come after us. But they would have to find another boat first, and it would have to have radar, and be fast, if they hoped to find us. I hadn't seen any boats like that on the beach, but there probably were some in boathouses, or under tarps. If they ever did manage to locate us, I would see them coming on radar first anyway, and we'd simply submerge and disappear. Unless they had sophisticated sonar, and a couple of very fast boats, and maybe a helicopter or plane, they were no threat to us on the sea.

But this was the first time I had made such a big decision without really thinking it through. There was so little time; I had to act. How could I not? I already *was* involved. I had witnessed their crime, and their dumping of the body, and had found their cache of weapons, drugs, and treasure. They were perfectly prepared to continue acts of piracy, to sell drugs, kill people, and who knew what else? If knowing that didn't make me responsible, what did? There had been a chance to take it all away from them, and so I took it. They never saw me coming or going. They would never even know what had happened.

Five miles from shore, I shut the engine off, climbed out, and jumped onto the sailboat. The sun was coming up. I went inside the cabin and looked around. It stank really badly, even worse than rotten fish. It made me feel like throwing up. There were at least three dozen guns of different types, and there were boxes of ammunition. Some of the guns were old, and some new. The bags of white powder looked like icing sugar, but must have been drugs. There were seven of those. There were six bundles of money wrapped in elastic bands. Two of the bundles looked like American twenty-dollar bills. The others were of different sizes and from countries I didn't know. Probably they were African. All of the money was dirty. The gold and jewellery in the heavy plastic bag was old and had come from the sea. Some of it was encrusted from lying in salt water for probably hundreds of years. There were coins, too. As I looked around, I knew what I had to do. I had to scuttle the boat.

What a strange feeling it was to step through the cabin, pick up the money, put it into the bag with the treasure, and carry it out. I felt like a criminal. On the other hand, I was stealing from pirates to try to stop them from hurting more people, or at least to make it harder for them. And that was surely the most responsible thing to do? I supposed I could have sent the money and treasure to the bottom of the sea, too. But why not use it for something good? Unlike guns and drugs, there was nothing bad about money itself.

I had to step over and around the guns and ammunition. I climbed out of the cabin, jumped onto the hull of the sub, and looked back. I had a sudden urge to throw the bag back onto the sailboat, to keep everything together. I looked down at it in my hand. The money had black spots on it that looked like dried blood. The other pirate had been murdered for this bag. This was blood money. I felt an urge to get rid of it right away, before it could bring me any more trouble. I even swung my arm a little, as if I would throw it back. But there was no sincerity in my swing. I didn't really want to do it. I wanted to keep it.

I wrapped the bag inside a burlap sack and hid it under the potatoes in the coldest compartment of the sub, my root cellar, where the crew wouldn't touch it. Then I heard a beep on the radar. A quick glance showed a vessel turning the north end of the island. They were coming. I watched the screen for a moment. They were coming fast. They must have found a speedboat. I had to hurry.

I grabbed the crowbar and a fifty-foot length of rope,

jumped to the sailboat, and smashed in the windows. That would let water in faster. Then I climbed part way up the mast and tied the rope as high as I could reach, just as the other pirate had done. I jumped back to the sub, started the engine, steered to the side of the sailboat, and pulled her over. When she was down, I shut the engine off, untied the rope from the mast, dropped it into the portal, grabbed the binoculars, and scanned the water. As I caught sight of them racing towards me, I saw two of the men in the boat holding binoculars and staring back. They had seen everything. It was time to go.

The sailboat started to sink quickly because the cabin filled with water right away. No doubt the weight of the guns and ammunition was helping to pull her down. She'd be under the water before they even reached the scene. So would we. I took a last look at her as she rolled over and exposed her keel. "I'm sorry," I said, as she began to pitch. I couldn't believe I was watching another boat go to the bottom of the sea, and this time I was the one sending her there. But there was no time to think of anything else. I took one last look at the approaching boat. I could see it clearly enough without binoculars now. The men were waving their arms wildly but apparently had no guns to shoot. I jumped inside the portal, shut the hatch, hit the dive switch, and submerged.

As we went down, so did the sailboat, though she fell more slowly. I didn't wait to watch her settle. I engaged the batteries, motored half a mile towards the island, and surfaced to periscope depth. I wanted to see what the pirates would do next.

Through the periscope, I saw their boat sitting in the water where the sailboat had gone down. They were standing up and staring at the water, but there was nothing they could see, and nothing they could do. Would they hunt me now, as they had hunted the other pirate? Of course they would. And if they ever found me, they would kill me, too.

But we weren't staying around. I wanted to sail to the Cape of Good Hope and see some of South Africa. I wanted to see zebras, ostriches, lions, elephants, giraffes, and rhinoceroses. My guidebook said there was a colony of penguins just south of Cape Town. I wanted to see that, too. And I felt confident that when we left this area, and sailed hundreds of miles due south, we'd never see these pirates again. But I never realized just how serious the pirate threat had become in Africa, how far south it had spread, or how persistent and vengeful pirates could really be. It wouldn't take long to find out.

It was two whole days of sailing before I dared to bring the crew to shore again. Hollie really needed to get out and run on the beach; he had been cooped up too long. Especially since Little Laura was sticking to him like glue. Whenever he slept, she crawled in against his belly where it was warm and slept too, or cleaned her feathers. Then she began climbing onto his back, and would hold on even when he walked around the sub. Her claws were small and sharp; he must have felt them through his fur, but he never complained. Still,

I saw that longing look in his eyes, to have the freedom of the beach to run wild.

And there was something I wanted to do on shore that I couldn't do on the sub because I didn't have enough fresh water—wash the money. It smelled like rotten stinky cheese. It also had blood stains on it. I wanted to count it, but before I could count it, I had to wash it. I knew you could wash money with water and soap because I had forgotten money in my pockets so many times when my pants went through the washing machine. If the money was too old, it might rip apart. If it was new, it was okay.

A couple of hundred miles south of Mozambique Island was another city called Angoche. My guidebook said it used to be a major slave-trading port. For hundreds of years, people were taken from their villages, forced onto ships, and sold into slavery. Looking at the pretty green land from the water, it was hard to imagine that happening here.

Angoche was bigger than Mozambique Island, and had a large river estuary. But I wouldn't risk mooring here because of the pirates. Instead, I chose a spot a little further south, where a smaller river emptied into the sea.

Before I inflated the kayak and rowed to shore with the crew, I checked with radar to make certain there were no vessels within ten miles of us. Then I put the money and some soap in the tool bag I always used for carrying Hollie around on land. It was a nylon mesh bag with a wooden frame, and hung from a strap over my shoulder. I hung the binoculars around my neck, let Seaweed out, inflated the kayak, and climbed in with Hollie. I shut the hatch with Little Laura inside. It was too soon and too risky to take her in the kayak.

I paddled about three hundred feet to the beach, pulled the kayak up on the sand, and let Hollie out. He ran like a convict who had just escaped from jail. "Don't run too far, Hollie! Stay close to me."

The river wasn't much more than a large ditch. It ran shallow over stones, and its banks were made of sand. But the water was fresh. I reached down, cupped my hand, and tasted it. I pulled the tool bag off my back, put it down, and lifted out the money. We had about half an hour to an hour at most. Anything longer and the sub might be discovered on radar by another vessel, and I wouldn't know. I had to wash the money as quickly as I could. Hollie wouldn't want to go so soon, I knew, but it really wasn't that safe being here in the first place.

I started to wash the American bills first. I pulled a handful out from the elastic bands, put them down on the sand, poured soap on them, picked up one, and the brush, and started scrubbing it quickly in the water. When it was clean, I put it down and grabbed another one. After I had done five, I raised my head and took a peek at the horizon with the binoculars. Then I dropped my head and washed five more. I raised my head every five bills, which was a hundred dollars.

It was tiring washing the money, and I soon realized it was going to take a lot longer than half an hour to do it all. Too bad there wasn't a washing machine that I could throw all the money inside. There probably wasn't a washing machine for five hundred miles of here. I wondered where the pirates were. I could imagine how angry they would be if they could see me now.

After the seventh pile of five bills, I raised my head to scan the water again, and got a heck of a fright. Half a dozen people were standing in the sand, staring at me. Hollie was standing next to them. I jumped to my feet. For a second, I thought they were the pirates, and an icy chill ran up my spine. But they weren't. They were just people who lived in the area. I could tell from the looks on their faces that they were as surprised to see me as I was to see them. Then they saw the money in my hands and on the sand beside me, and their eyes opened wider.

There was an older man who was probably the father, a woman, a younger woman, and three boys. I smiled and waved, and they smiled and waved back. "Hello!" I said. The father said something back. They couldn't take their eyes off the money. It felt awkward. I didn't know what else to do so I reached down and picked up one of the American twenties and a handful of bills from one of the African piles. "Would you like some?" I said. I reached it towards him.

They stared at me as if I were crazy. The father stepped closer and looked at the bills. Suddenly he jumped back as if something had bitten him. I think he saw the spots of dried blood on the money. He started speaking loudly and turned around and opened his arms wide, trying to gather his family together. They all looked frightened to death. Then, they turned around and ran away. I watched them run across the sand and disappear beneath the palm trees. They never even looked back. Why were they so afraid? It was only money. Surely they didn't think I was a pirate?

# Chapter Nine

I CLEANED A THOUSAND dollars before returning to the sub. Cleaning money was a lot of work, and was really boring. Judging from the size of the piles, I was guessing I had about twenty thousand dollars in American bills. Two of the other piles were South African rand. Two were from Nigeria. Handling it made me feel sick, it stank so badly. I put the thousand dollars in my money tin and the rest of the money back into the burlap sack and shoved it under the potatoes.

The treasure didn't stink. It had lain under the sea for hundreds of years, so even though it was encrusted, it was clean, and smelled clean. There were seventeen gold coins, Spanish or Portuguese, I didn't know which. There were three large gold rings, two gold necklaces with pearls, diamonds, rubies, and emeralds on them, and two large gold bracelets with similar jewels. It was a small treasure, but I bet it was worth a lot of money. All of it fit into three of my tea tins. I wrapped it in plastic bags and put the rest of the tea on top to hide it. But then the tins weighed a ton. If anyone picked them up, they would know right away there was more than tea inside them. So, I spread the treasure out. I wrapped each individual piece in a small plastic bag, and buried it under the tea, coffee, sugar, oats, beans, spices, jam, and peanut butter. Then I tried to forget about it.

The money was different. It stank so badly it was ruining the potatoes, although maybe the potatoes were going bad anyway. I had to keep that compartment shut. I planned to use some of the money to buy fresh fruit and vegetables as soon as I had the chance. But I had to find a way to clean the rest of it first, before the whole sub started to stink. Even when I tried to sleep I could smell it, the scent of stinky cheese. It made you want to clear your throat all the time. I had to cover my nose to fall asleep.

A hundred miles further south, I stopped again. Where the Ligonha River emptied into the sea, according to my map, there wasn't a town or city, just a river basin, and I doubted the pirates would bother to stop there, unless of course they knew I was there. To be extra careful, I sailed the last twenty miles submerged, just in case they had somehow gotten their hands on radar more sophisticated than mine, which was pretty unlikely. And when I surfaced—two hundred feet from shore—I brought the portal only eight inches above water, leaving the hull submerged, so that we'd be nearly invisible by radar and by sight. You would have to scan the shore with a high-powered telescope to see the portal, and even then you might not know it was a submarine. And who would ever be looking *that* closely?

This time I decided to bring Little Laura along. I put a piece of orange inside her cage, and when she went in for it, I shut the door. I inflated the kayak, took Hollie, the money, the cage, the binoculars, and paddled to the beach. Seaweed was already there.

It was a pretty river basin. The river cut several trenches through the sandy soil, making little islands out of the beach. The sand was golden, the trees bright green, and the water in the river clear and blue. There was no one around, which suited me perfectly. I pulled the kayak onto the beach, and carried the money and cage upstream along the river to a good spot for cleaning.

Hollie ran wild as usual. Seaweed investigated the riverbank for things to eat. Little Laura looked all around from inside her cage, but wouldn't come out. I opened the door and she poked her head out, but stayed inside. She stared at Hollie as if waiting for him to come and carry her around, but there was no way on earth he would give up his freedom on the beach to offer her a piggyback ride. I settled down on the riverbank with a brush and soap and started scrubbing the money.

Who knew cleaning money would be so much work? I couldn't help wondering how it got so dirty in the first place. Had it passed through so many dirty hands? But the money wasn't old. Most of it looked fairly new. Had it sat around in a room with sour milk that slowly turned into rotten cheese? But it wasn't exactly a cheese smell; it was stinkier than that. Then I imagined even worse things. Had the money been buried in the ground for a while, with a dead body or two? Stop thinking like that, I told myself, it was just dirty. But the more I handled the money, the dirtier it felt, and the harder I scrubbed it.

There was a fresh breeze coming across the land. This was very welcome to me because the smell of the money was making me sick. I raised my head to look at the sea, but couldn't see it. I had to stand up. When I did, the horizon was clear. No one knew we were here. I looked around. This was such a pleasant place; it was hard to believe that people were taken from here and sold into slavery. But they were. They went mostly to the Caribbean and America, but other places, too. What really surprised me was that the slave traders didn't have to come inland to raid the villages themselves; they were able to buy the people from tribal chiefs. The chiefs sold their own people, or people from neighbouring tribes, to the traders. I didn't know which would be worse: being kidnapped by strangers, or being sold by your own people.

Probably being sold by your own people. The reason was the same in both cases—for money.

As I scrubbed each bill, turned it over, and scrubbed the other side, I thought of the family who had run away from me when they saw the money. Why had they been so afraid? Money was just money. It wasn't evil. I stood up and scanned the horizon again. As I stared at the vast hazy ocean, I imagined old wooden sailing ships coming in and dropping anchor. Sailors would come ashore in rowboats, greet the tribal chiefs, and hand over money for slaves . . . I stopped. That was it. I remembered watching shows about the pirates in Somalia. It was the tribal chiefs who forced the young men into piracy—their own people—just as their ancestors had sold their own people to slave traders. No wonder people would be afraid of money around here. In their past, and in their present, their own chiefs were willing to trade them, or force them into a violent and dangerous life, just to make money. Now I understood why the sight of someone washing blood off money would have been frightening to a poor local family.

I cleaned another thousand dollars. My hands were tired now, and a little sore. The brush was rubbing the skin away from my fingernails and making them bleed. What a nuisance. On the other hand, I was a thousand dollars richer. I stood up to stretch my back and take another peek at the horizon. It was clear. Then, I looked at the portal of the sub. Strangely, it looked a little fatter than before. How could that be? I grabbed the binoculars and looked more closely. Directly behind the portal, near the horizon, was a motorboat, and it was coming fast. They had found us.

I grabbed the money and Little Laura's cage. "Hollie! We have to go! Hollie?"

I didn't see him. Where was he? I ran to the kayak. "Hollie!"

The pirates were only three or four miles away. They would be here in minutes. I dropped the cage and money into the kayak and pushed it into the water. Where was Hollie? We had to go *now*. If the pirates caught us, we were dead. "Hollie!"

He didn't come. I couldn't see Seaweed, either. I started to feel panic. I hated to go without Hollie, but would have to come back and find him later; otherwise, we'd both be dead. So, I paddled to the sub, opened the hatch, and carried Little Laura and the money inside. Then I climbed back out. There was a sound of a rifle shot in the distance, but it was far away. I raised the binoculars. It was the pirates all right. They were crowded in the boat, with guns in their arms. One of them was aiming, but couldn't hit us from so far away, especially from a moving boat. I pulled up the anchor and prepared to shut the hatch. Now only my head was showing. I took a glance at the beach, and then I saw Hollie. He was in the water, swimming towards the sub. But he was too slow. "Hurry! Hollie! Hurry!"

There was no way he could make it here in time. I looked at the pirates. We had maybe a minute and a half at most. With a horrible sinking feeling, I climbed out, slipped into the water, and swam to Hollie as fast as I could. I grabbed him by the back of his neck and struggled back. There were more rifle shots now, and they were louder. Instead of climbing up the portal and exposing my body, I slithered inside like a snake, headfirst, holding Hollie in one hand. I went in upside down, bracing myself with the ladder, and let Hollie drop the last couple of feet. I closed the hatch, raced to the panel board, and hit the dive and battery switches all at the same time. Before we went under, I heard a bullet strike the portal.

I hoped they didn't have grenades. If they did, they could cause us a lot of trouble as we went underneath them. The water was so shallow they would be able to follow us easily for a mile from the beach, until the sea floor dropped. And that is what they did. They followed us out, shooting the whole time. I tracked them with sonar, and could hear the faint sounds of gunshots. They were shooting into the water, even though it was useless for them. The bullets lost most of their power once they hit the water, and couldn't hurt the steel hull anyway. They must have been wild with anger. Thank heavens they didn't have grenades. Still, I sat at the control panel and shivered. It had been way too close. If I hadn't looked for them just then, we'd probably be dead now. I just couldn't take any more chances like that. We would sail away from here now, once we had picked up Seaweed. We would sail far away, and never come back.

Three miles from shore, I surfaced to periscope depth and scanned the water. The pirates were racing in circles, trying desperately to find us. I watched them for an hour. Sooner or later, they would get frustrated and give up. Then we could go back and find Seaweed. He could spot the periscope for miles from the sky. After we picked him up, we'd sail hundreds of miles away before we set foot on shore again. I didn't think the pirates would follow us that far. They couldn't follow us forever.

# Chapter Ten

HUNDREDS OF MILES south, just south of Maputo, we were sitting in the water a few miles offshore. It was the middle of the afternoon, sunny and hot, with a very slight breeze passing over the open hatch. I was making pancakes, with raspberry jam and maple syrup. I could finally flip a pancake in the air and catch it in the pan without breaking it or dropping it on the floor. Seaweed, Hollie, and Little Laura were standing by my feet, watching every move, and hoping I would drop one. The air was a little smoky. The sub smelled a bit like a restaurant, which was a huge improvement.

I had just sat down and taken the first bite when the radar

beeped. I glanced over and saw the light blinking on the screen. There had been surprisingly few vessels in the water all along the Mozambique coast, and I had gone out of my way to avoid them these past few days. But this vessel wasn't coming from the north or south, it was coming from shore.

I put my plate down, picked up the binoculars, climbed the ladder, and scanned the water. There was nothing there. Not a thing. That was weird. I ducked my head inside and listened. The radar was still beeping. So, I looked more carefully, drawing the binoculars along the shoreline very slowly. Nope. There was nothing there. What the heck?

I jumped back inside and took another look at the radar screen. Whatever had been three miles away from us was now just a mile. The only thing that could move that fast was an airplane, or a helicopter. But I never heard one. I raced back up the portal and scanned the sky. Yup. There it was.

It was sort of an airplane. I couldn't tell if it was really old, or really new. There was someone in it, but he wasn't covered. He was pedalling with his legs, and swinging levers with his arms. There was a small engine in front, a propeller, and a pair of wings that looked like they were made of canvas. In the centre was a bicycle. He was pedalling as if he were in a race. But he was losing. The plane was coming down. He was going to hit the water.

At first he didn't see me, until I waved with both of my arms over my head. And then he did. He made an awkward turn, losing more height, and steered towards us. But he wasn't going to make it. I couldn't hear his engine because it wasn't running. He was pedalling faster and faster, trying to stay aloft. The bicycle must have been hooked up to the propeller, and it was spinning, but it wasn't enough to keep him in the air.

I watched him drift closer. He looked frantic. I wondered if he could swim. I jumped inside, switched on the engine, and motored towards him. Just as I poked my head out of the portal again, he plunged into the sea. He dropped like a dead bird.

His plane didn't sink right away, and he was clinging to it like somebody who couldn't swim. As we approached, I cut the engine and drifted to a stop. He was staring at me with a mix of panic and curiosity. He was a few years older than me. "Are you okay," I yelled?

He didn't answer. He was trying to untangle himself. That was a good idea; his plane was going to sink. I grabbed the lifebuoy. "Do you want this?"

He looked up. "Is that a diesel-electric submarine?"

"Yes."

He wrestled free of his contraption, but never took his eyes away from the sub. "Where are you from?"

"Canada."

"Canada? What are you . . . ?"

"Can you swim?"

"No." He said it as if it was not important. I threw the lifebuoy at him. "Here. Pull it over your head and I'll haul you over."

He pulled the lifebuoy over one shoulder and began thrashing at the water. I yanked hard on the rope. He tried to swim, in a panicky sort of way, but it was as if he didn't even know what water was. His eyes were wild with panic, like an animal, yet he couldn't seem to take them away from the sub. It was the worst attempt at swimming I had ever seen. He wouldn't have gone anywhere but straight down if I hadn't been pulling on the rope.

By the time he reached a handle and climbed halfway up, he was exhausted. I waited for him to catch his breath. When he did, he continued talking, as if he had never stopped. "Are you burning diesel fuel?"

"Of course. It's a diesel engine."

"You don't have to, you know. You can convert it."

"Convert it? Convert what?"

"Your engine. You don't have to burn fossil fuels anymore. You can burn vegetable fat."

"Vegetable fat? Are you serious?"

"Absolutely. My engine burns vegetable fat. It's a lot better for the environment. Why would you burn diesel when you can burn vegetable fat? It's cleaner, and it's renewable. We have to stop burning fossil fuels. We're killing the planet. And we haven't got much time left." He bent over and gasped for air. "Will you tow my plane to the shore?"

I shook my head. "Sorry. I can't."

"Why not?"

"Because it sank."

"No, it didn't . . ." He turned around. "Oh, no! Noooooooo!"

"Sorry."

"I . . . I have to get it back!" He jumped back into the water and splashed around. He ducked his head under and looked down, but didn't take a breath first. When his head came up, he was choking and spitting up water. I was starting to wonder if this was his very first time on the sea. He acted as if he didn't even know what it was.

I pulled on the rope again until he grabbed hold of the side of the sub. He looked so disappointed now you would have thought that somebody had just died. I didn't think I had ever seen anyone look so disappointed before. I couldn't help feeling sorry for him.

"I might be able to find it for you, if the salt water hasn't ruined it."

He looked up. "Really? How could you do that?"

"Well, it's only ninety feet deep. I could swim down with a rope and hook, and we could pull it up. It's possible. But I think the salt water probably ruined your engine."

"No. I can clean it. I built it from scratch. I can take it apart and clean it." He turned and stared at the water as if he expected his plane to come back up all by itself. Then he shifted his weight, lost his balance, and fell into the water again. Oh boy. When I helped him out, he was spitting up water. I think he was completely exhausted now. Maybe he was hungry, too.

"Are you hungry?"

He raised his head and looked at me as if food was something he hadn't thought of for a very long time. He suddenly looked very tired, sad, and lonely. "Yah. I'm starving."

"I'm making pancakes. Would you like some?"

"I'm not sure what they are, but I'll eat them."

I reached down and offered him my hand. "I'm Alfred."

He reached up. His hand was shaking. His lips were turning blue. He was shivering. "I'm Los."

"Are you okay?"

He nodded, but he wasn't okay. He was shaking. I think maybe he really was starving.

"Come on in. I'll give you something to eat."

He followed me. Just before he dropped his head inside the portal, he stopped and stared at the shore. He had a curious and dreamy look on his face. "We're on the sea, aren't we?"

"Yes."

"Wow." He climbed down the ladder. "And this is really a submarine, isn't it?"

"Yes, it is."

Inside the sub, Los looked like a kid who had just come into a toy store for the very first time. Even though he was exhausted, and starving, he examined everything with intense curiosity. He couldn't help it. I could tell that he was someone whose energy came from his mind, not his body. In a funny way, he reminded me of Albert Einstein.

"This is amazing. You've got to show me how everything works." When he stood up, his head was almost touching the ceiling. He was about two inches taller than me, and maybe a little slimmer.

"Sure. I will, right after we eat . . . Oh!" My pancake wasn't on my plate anymore. I looked on the floor. It wasn't there, either, but there was a sticky streak of raspberry jam. I looked at the crew. They were standing apart from each other and staring at me. I wondered which one had taken it. Probably Seaweed. But they all looked guilty. "Never mind. I'll cook some fresh ones. This is my crew. This is Hollie." Hollie came over and sniffed Los, who bent down and touched him on the head. It wasn't really a pat; it was more of a poke, to see if he was real. "This is Seaweed." Seaweed completely ignored Los because he wasn't carrying food. It was probably the height of rudeness in the seagull world to meet someone for the first time and not bring food. "And this is Little Laura. She just joined us last week." Little Laura took a few steps sideways, until she was next to Hollie. She opened her mouth and made the little swallowing movements she always made just after she had eaten. She was definitely guilty.

I made a double batch of pancakes, and Los ate the whole thing, drank four glasses of water, and a whole pot of tea! As soon as he finished one pancake, I put another one on his plate, and he gobbled it up as if it were his very first meal. I had never seen anyone eat like that before.

"This is really good!" he said. He never even slowed down. But after a while, his eyes began to droop. Still, he pushed himself to eat, as if he believed he wouldn't get a chance to eat again for a long time. I had given him a sleeping bag to sit on, beside Hollie. But when I went into the stern to dig through the dry supplies for more powdered milk, and came back, he was lying sideways on the bag, curled up and fast asleep.

I made another plate of pancakes for myself, and ate them as I watched Los sleep, and listened to him snore. I knew what it was like to be that exhausted. He would probably sleep for a long time. I wondered how long he had been flying before he crashed into the sea. And how he got into the air in the first place. Did he push his plane off a mountain? His crash reminded me of the story of Icarus, who flew too close to the sun with wings made of feathers and wax. When the sun melted the wax, Icarus plunged to his death in the sea. I wondered if that's why Los had been shaking so much— he had just realized that his plane didn't float, and he couldn't swim. If we hadn't been in the water nearby, he would have drowned. I knew that shaky feeling too, of being close to death. It wasn't very nice.

As I watched him sleeping on the floor, snoring like a goat, something about him unsettled me, though I didn't know what it was. It was only after I stopped trying to figure it out that it came to me. It was his recklessness. He was obviously very smart, inventive, and good at building things. But he had come through the air in a machine that couldn't stay aloft once it had run out of fuel. And he flew it over the sea, where he couldn't land, and when he had no flotation devices, and couldn't swim. Not only that, he had come without food or water. Had he given no thought to any of those things? Had he no help or advice from anyone? At first glance, he had looked so cool in his flying machine. In reality, it had been practically a suicide mission. Here, now, he was asleep on the floor of a vessel of someone he didn't know at all.

What if I were a pirate? There were lots of them around here. What if I killed him in his sleep? Why would he trust me so quickly? He was probably nineteen or twenty years old, but I had the feeling he might not live very long.

# Chapter Eleven

HE SLEPT THE REST of the day and night, snoring the whole time. When I brought a pillow out and put it under his head, he didn't wake. The crew stepped around him as if he were a piece of driftwood we had carried in from the beach. Hollie sniffed him every time he went around him, trying to identify smells he had never smelled before. And Los did have a particular smell, like a spice or herb, like wild garlic. It was a good smell.

While he slept, I found his plane. It was an unmistakable shape on sonar ninety feet below. I steered the sub until we were directly above it, then dropped a hundred-foot rope over the side, with a hook to pull it down. I took a careful look at Los to make sure he was still asleep, climbed out, slipped into the water, took a few breaths, and went down.

I was glad for the chance to practise diving. If you don't practise holding your breath under water, you lose your ability to do it. On the way down, I looked for sharks. My guide-book said that the seas of South Africa were thick with sharks, dolphins and whales. I had seen lots of sharks in my travels. Most were just curious, like fish. And the aggressive ones, like tiger sharks, would only eat you if you gave them an invita-tion. I didn't see any on the way down.

It was murky at the bottom. There was a current stirring up a fine silt. I had no problem finding the plane, but couldn't tell if it was upside down or not. The silt was creeping over it like snow drifting over old farm machinery in a field. It would be covered in no time. I wrapped the hook around a bar in the centre, and pulled it through a loop in the rope. Then I turned around and headed back up. There were a couple of dark shapes in the distance. Probably they were sharks, but as I wasn't moving with panic, and wasn't bleeding, they never bothered me.

Back on the sub, I pulled the slackness out of the rope and felt the weight of the machine. It was pretty heavy. I could lift it if I had to, but it would take a long time, and I'd get lots of blisters. I decided to wait for Los to wake up. But how would we tow it to shore when the water was so shallow? We'd have to figure that out. In the meantime, I thought I should get some sleep, too. I lay down on my hanging cot and drifted off, listening to Los snore and the crew shuffle around him. I slept very lightly, half listening for Los to wake, and half listening for a beep on the radar. If any vessels were coming our way, I needed to know who they were.

Seven hours later, I hopped out of bed. Los still hadn't moved. I put the kettle on and fed the crew. They weren't happy having to step around someone sleeping in their space. Hollie didn't mind, but Seaweed and Little Laura were not impressed at all. I think they would have pushed him over the side if they could.

I put a pot on for porridge and sat down with a cup of tea and my book—Joseph Conrad's *Heart of Darkness*. It was the story of a British sailor who travelled up a river in Africa to find a man who went crazy. It was dark and savage, full of greed and violence, and I didn't really like it. But it had been a gift from Sheba, one of my two favourite people in the world, so I felt I should read it. I was just glad I wasn't visiting Africa at a time like that. Then I thought for a minute; maybe it wasn't all that different today.

Hollie's tail started wagging when Los moved. Little Laura scampered up the rope to her cage. Seaweed climbed the ladder and hopped into the air. The sun had been up for a while. It shone into the water and came up through the observation window in the floor. Los' eyes opened slowly, like a lizard's, and he stared blindly, as if he were waking from a faraway dream.

"Good morning," I said.

He didn't answer right away. I think he couldn't remember where he was. He rubbed his eyes. "Are we in a submarine?"

"Yes."

"Wow. Is it your submarine?"

"Yes."

"Is there anybody else?"

"Just my crew." I pointed to Hollie and Little Laura.

He sat up and looked around. "Is this where you live?"

"Pretty much. I really live in Canada, but I'm at sea most of the time."

He stared sleepily as his eyes drifted across the control panel, the sonar and radar screens, the periscope, bicycle, hanging cot, air-compressors, valves, gauges, pipes running everywhere. Gradually, the sleepiness in his eyes faded, and was replaced by a look of desire. I knew that desire well, the desire for the freedom and capability that well-functioning machines could give you, though I couldn't help wondering if his desire knew no caution. I also thought I saw frustration in his eyes, like someone who had learned everything the hard way, and was tired of learning that way.

"Where did you get it?"

"My sub? My friend and I built it. Well, he built it. I just helped him. His name is Ziegfried."

"How long did it take?"

"Two and a half years."

"Was it hard?"

"I guess so. It was a lot of work, that's for sure. But I think the hardest part was probably just the waiting until it was finished. Ziegfried is extremely concerned with safety, and he had to test everything over and over and over. I found that hard. But if he hadn't done it, I probably wouldn't be here now. He works with the belief that anything that can go wrong, will, sooner or later. I've already learned that he was right about that."

"He sounds pretty smart."

"He is. Actually, he's a genius."

"But how could he build a submarine? Where did he get all the materials?"

"He owns a junkyard. That's where we built it. We started with an old oil tank. First we reinforced the steel; then we built the wooden interior. There's a complicated hardwood frame beneath this cedar and pine that supports the hull against water pressure. There is also a thick layer of rubber between the wood and steel. The sub is designed to bounce when it hits something, instead of cracking and leaking. It really works, too. I learned that when I sailed through the Arctic and hit lots of ice."

"That's amazing. If I went to Canada, would he help me build one?"

Los' question took me by surprise. "Uhh . . . I don't know. Maybe."

"Do you *think* he would help me?"

"It's possible. But I can't really say. I can't speak for him. I think he'd respect you for building your own flying machine, but he'd think you were crazy for flying it over the sea, especially when you can't swim. Ziegfried is so big on safety he wouldn't help you if he thought you were going to be reckless once you went to sea. If something happened to you, he would feel responsible."

"What do you mean by reckless?"

"It means not being careful enough."

"I never planned to fly over the sea! There was nowhere to land! The dry ground ended and there was nothing but trees and swamp. I couldn't land there. I was hoping to turn around and go back. And then, I hoped to land on the beach."

"Did you run out of gas?"

"I don't burn gas. I burn vegetable fat. Yes, I ran out of fuel a long time ago. But I was pedalling okay until I reached the sea. Then the air pushed me down. It wasn't my fault. I did everything right. Will you help me find my plane?"

"I found it. And tied a rope to it. We can pull it up."

"You found it? That's great!"

"We can pull it up, but I don't know how to get it to shore. The water is too shallow for the sub. I have an inflatable kayak, but I don't know if it's big enough to hold your plane."

"I saw a city from the air. We could tow it there."

"Maputo? I'm trying to avoid places like that right now. There are people chasing me."

"It's not Maputo. Maputo is in Mozambique. We are in South Africa. It's Richards Bay."

"No, it isn't. It's Maputo. Mozambique. Why do you think we are in South Africa?"

"Because we are! That's where I'm from." He looked worried. "It *has* to be South Africa. I have no papers for Mozambique. If they found me, they would put me in jail, and I would never get out. It's Richards Bay. I flew exactly east."

"Well, I am sorry to tell you that we are in Mozambique. You must have flown northeast. Don't you have a compass on your plane?"

"No."

Somehow that didn't surprise me. "Well, don't worry. I don't have papers, either. And I can take you to South Africa. That's where I am going."

"But who is chasing you?"

"Pirates. I had a few run-ins with them a couple of hundred miles north. They've been following me ever since. If they find me, they will kill me."

"Why? What did you do to them?"

"I took something of theirs. Well, it wasn't really theirs, but I took it."

"You robbed pirates? Are you crazy? What did you steal?"

"It wasn't really stealing. I took things that they had taken from other people. I was trying to stop them from hurting more people."

Los' eyes opened wide. "Did you take guns?"

"I didn't actually take them. I sank their boat. I sent it to the bottom with all of their guns and drugs. But now they have another boat, with more guns, and they are trying to find me."

He shook his head at me, but spoke in a softer voice. "You are a dead man, Alfred. They will follow you forever."

"No, I'm not. They can do all they want; they will never catch me. I won't be staying around here. And they can't follow me across the sea. It's impossible."

Los paused. "You can sail across the sea, can't you?"

"Yes, I can."

"That is amazing."

"Yes, it is."

"Will you help me raise my airplane out of the sea now?"

"Sure."

So we climbed out, and I handed him a life jacket. "Here! You have to put this on. Just in case you fall in."

"No. I won't need that. I have good balance."

"It doesn't matter. You have to wear it anyway. You can't swim."

"No, I'm okay."

Gosh, he was stubborn. "Look. I am the captain of this submarine. As long as you are on board my submarine, you have to obey my orders. That's how it works. That's the Law of the Sea. Now, I *order* you to put on this life jacket."

"You are ordering me?"

"Yes. For your own good. If you don't like it, I will take you to shore, and you can find your own airplane, and take it to South Africa by yourself."

He stared at me to see if I was bluffing. I wasn't. "It's for your own safety. If you fall in, I might not be able to save you, and you will drown because you cannot swim. Drowning means dying. Do you understand that?" I wasn't certain he did. I also wasn't certain if I liked him yet or not. I sort of did, but he was so darn stubborn.

He grabbed the jacket and put it on. "Everybody dies sometime."

"Yes, but you don't have to die today. And I'd prefer if you didn't die on my submarine."

"I'm not afraid of dying."

"I can tell."

When Los had the jacket strapped on, we stood side by side and started pulling up the rope. Every time we raised eight feet or so, we wrapped a loop around the portal, so we could stop and rest without dropping the plane. It was easier together, but still a lot of work. When the plane was about halfway up, we stopped, rested for a minute, and stared at the shore. I wondered where he was from, and how he had come to build his own plane. Where did he learn how? Did he teach himself? I got the feeling he was on his own. He just gave me that impression. I was guessing we had a few things in common.

When the plane was almost in sight, Los asked me casually what that sound was. I had injured my ears in India, and they weren't completely healed yet. Sometimes I had a ringing in them. "What sound?"

"That beeping sound."

I stopped and listened. Suddenly, I knew what it was even before I heard it—the radar. I raised my head above the portal and glanced towards the horizon. Two motorboats were racing towards us at top speed. They looked like flying fish. I didn't need binoculars to know who they were.

# Chapter Twelve

"WE HAVE TO GO! *Now!* Come on!"

"No! I can't leave my plane. We almost have it."

"We have to leave it. I'm sorry. We'll come back for it later. We have to untie it and let it go."

"No! I am not dropping it again."

I jumped inside, grabbed the binoculars, climbed out, and took a closer look at the approaching boats. They were pirates all right. There were more of them now, and they had guns. I couldn't tell if they were the same ones I had seen before, but they were definitely looking for us. "Los! We have to leave *now*! Do you want to get killed?"

"I almost have it!" He continued pulling the rope by himself, but the life jacket was getting in his way, so he took it off and threw it onto the hull. "It's right here! I can see it!"

"I'm sorry. We can't take it with us. We have to get inside!"

"No! Not without my plane."

I looked at the boats. They were racing towards us as fast as they could. We had maybe two or three minutes at the most. I looked at Los. He was trying to hook the rope onto a handle on the hull. That was crazy. The plane would slow us down terribly, and the movement through the water would probably rip the plane apart anyway. "Los! Look!" I came over and handed him the binoculars. "Take a look!"

He didn't want to. "I have to save my plane . . ."

"*Look!* I order you to look!"

"Order yourself! I'm saving my plane."

I grabbed the rope with one hand and pulled it away from him. With the other hand, I shoved the binoculars against him. He almost fell off the hull. "Okay, okay. I will look." He raised the binoculars awkwardly and tried to look at the water. I reached over and pulled them around so that they were pointing towards the approaching boats. He stared for a long time.

"Do you see them?"

He nodded, lowered the binoculars, turned, and looked at me with pain in his eyes. "We are going to die."

"No, we are not going to die. Drop the rope and get inside."

It didn't take any more coaxing once he saw what was

coming. As he climbed into the portal and went down the ladder, I pulled the rope taut and cut it. I could have untied it, but I'd rather lose ten feet of rope instead of a hundred. Maybe we'd find the plane again, and maybe we wouldn't. I tried to fix an exact imprint of the shoreline in my mind before jumping inside the portal and shutting the hatch. I heard shots ring out just before I sealed it.

The pirates came spinning around us in their speedboats, though from inside the sub, their motors sounded like the motors of electric can openers. I flipped the dive switch and engaged battery power. Before we had gone far, we heard a loud explosion and the ping of metal shards striking the hull. "What was that?" Los asked.

"A grenade."

"Do you think they will sink us?"

"No, not unless we sit still and wait for them to drop more. But we're not going to do that; we're getting out of here. I doubt they have sonar."

"How can you tell?"

"If they can follow us when they can no longer see us. We'll know soon enough."

There were four more explosions—one close, and three further away. I steered straight out to sea, following the sea floor down from ninety feet to two hundred, then two-fifty, and then three hundred. At three hundred feet, I turned sharply to starboard and swung in a wide arc, very gradually coming around towards shore. Sonar revealed the pirates continued straight. They were chasing us blindly. They'd have more luck finding the *Titanic* than a moving submarine.

Los stood in the bow, holding on to a beam in the ceiling, and just watched as I pumped air into the tanks to rise back to periscope depth.

"Are they gone?"

"I don't know. They might be waiting, hoping to spot us, or they might think we're heading further south and follow us there. That's probably what they'll do. But I wonder if they'll follow us into South African waters. I don't think these were the guys who chased me before. They must have been told to search for me. I wonder how long they'll keep chasing me."

"Forever!"

"I don't think so. Sooner or later they'll realize they can't catch me. And surely they've got other things to do."

"But you took their drugs and their guns."

"I know."

"Did you take money, too?"

"Yes."

"Very much money?"

I shrugged. "I don't know. I didn't count it. It's mostly African money, and it's very dirty. It has blood stains on it."

Los swung his head from side to side. "You don't understand, Alfred. They have to find you and get their money back, or they will die. They are just doing what they are told to do. They have a chief, and their chief will kill them if they fail. That's the way it works. Pirates are a big problem in Africa now. Every week, people are taken hostage. If they don't get money, they kill them. And they sell drugs and guns, and make people afraid everywhere. Before, those men would kill you for a very small amount of money. Now that you have stolen from them, they *have* to find you and kill you or they will die themselves. That is how it works."

"Oh." It was more complicated than I thought. I wondered if I should try to return their money, so they wouldn't be killed. But how? And I couldn't return their drugs or guns, or their boat. And I wouldn't give back the drugs and guns anyway. And if I did give back the money, wouldn't their chief just use it to buy more drugs and guns?

"There is blood on the money?"

"Yes."

Now, Los looked sad. "Money is evil. It creates poverty and unhappiness. That's the truth. Only a few people get rich; the rest live in poverty. Money creates greed, and greed brings poverty, because the rich people won't share their money. They never do. Poverty brings desperation, and desperation brings violence. Money is a curse. You became cursed when you took it, Alfred."

"I don't believe that."

"You don't have to believe it to make it true."

Five feet from the surface, I let a little water into the tanks to stop rising. I raised the periscope and scanned the horizon. The two boats were about four miles away. They had split up to search for us. But it was hopeless for them. And now they couldn't go back until they had found what I had taken from them. Part of me felt badly about that. But then I remembered them killing the other pirate, and I didn't feel so badly anymore. Maybe they had been forced into piracy, but it was hard to feel sorry for them after witnessing that. Did they really have to kill people? I found that hard to believe. If I had been forced into piracy when I was only twelve, I would have run away at the first chance. I knew I would have. I just couldn't imagine anything else. I watched until the boats eventually disappeared around the point. They were heading further south.

"Are they gone?"

"Yes. For now."

"Do you think we can find my plane again?"

"We can try."

So we searched until we found the plane again. It only took an hour. Then, while Los kept an eye on the horizon with the binoculars, I dove down and retied the rope. Together, we raised it, but never took our eyes from the horizon. Once the plane was partly out of the water, we inflated the kayak and shoved it underneath. The kayak held the plane on the surface, though it sat at an awkward angle. I attached a line, and we towed the plane behind the sub.

We went down the coast very slowly, hugging the shore as closely as possible. Los wanted to hide the plane on land, somewhere where no one would ever find it. And it had to be reachable by car or truck. His plan was to borrow a truck, or a car with a trailer, and come and retrieve it. It also had to be a spot that he could find again.

After several hours of searching, he chose a spot. There were three palm trees close together at the mouth of a tiny river. Between the trees was a long narrow depression in the ground. It was very isolated. With wrenches from the sub, we removed the wings and rudder from the plane and tucked them in on top of the rest of it, and covered the whole thing with driftwood and palm tree branches. It wouldn't be the easiest place to reach with a car, but the plane could be carried out in pieces. Los was satisfied. We fixed the spot in our memories, and left.

Back on the sub, we headed south. Los sat on the floor in the bow and was quiet for a while. I could tell he was thinking about something. Finally, it came out.

"Alfred. Will you show me how to work the sub? Will you tell me how you built it? I want to know everything. I want to build my own submarine."

Oh boy. He didn't know what he was asking. "Well, I can show you how it works. And I can explain how we built it, but there is so much more to it than that. It would take you years to build one. And you would need special tools, and a place to build it, and hide it, and so many materials. I don't see how it would be possible by yourself. Where would you build it? And you would need a large tank. Do you know where you could get a tank?"

"Maybe. I have a friend in Ladysmith. She has a barn behind her house. That is where I build things, and where I sleep. It's my workshop. There is a junkyard outside of town. Maybe I could find a tank there. I have tools already. I could do it. I know I could. Would you come to Ladysmith and help me get started?"

"Come to Ladysmith?" My first thought was no. I didn't see how Los could build a submarine by himself. Yes, he had built his own plane, and that was pretty amazing, but a submarine was so much more work, and would take a lot more material. Ziegfried was able to build one not only because he was a genius, had years of experience working with metal, and owned every tool there was to own; he also had his own junkyard filled with metal and machinery. What he didn't have, he traded for. All of this just didn't seem realistic for Los.

And yet, as I listened to him, and saw the eagerness in his face, I remembered the feeling I had when I first spied the old tank in Ziegfried's junkyard through a hole in the fence. I was only twelve. And when I asked Ziegfried—a complete stranger to me then—if we could turn that tank into a submarine, unbelievably, he didn't laugh at me and say no, like anyone else in the world would have. He thought about it first. Then, once he started thinking about it, he couldn't stop. Two and a half years later, I went to sea in my own submarine. Here, now, Los was asking me to help him with the same dream. Many things were different, for sure, but it was more or less the same dream. How could I say no?

"Where is Ladysmith?"

"Not far. Two hundred and fifty kilometres."

"That's a hundred and fifty miles. How would we get there?"

"We could walk."

"No way! It would take forever. Besides, I have my crew. And where would I hide my sub?"

"We could buy a car with your stolen money. An old car. They are very cheap if you have money."

"I've never driven a car before. Have you?"

"Of course."

"I don't know. I have to think about it. What is the land like from here to there?"

"It is flat at first. And green, like here, with swamps and trees. And there are elephants and hippos."

"Elephants?"

"Yes. Then the ground turns dry and brown, and there are zebra and ostrich. Near Ladysmith there are mountains."

"It sounds interesting."

"It is very interesting. And my friend Katharina is there. She is the most wonderful woman in the world. She has saved me many times."

"From what?"

He hesitated. "From other people."

"I don't know. I'll have to think about it. First, we have to sail to South Africa."

Los smiled as if I had already agreed. "You will be happy you came."

"I didn't say yes yet. I don't even know if we could find a place to hide the sub."

"We will. You will see. You will be happy you came."

I wasn't so sure. I didn't feel confident about hiding the sub. The water was so shallow everywhere. And what about the pirates? On the other hand, I'd love to see some of the land. And I'd sure love to see elephants.

"Alfred?"

"Yes?"

"Can I ask you something else?"

"What?"

"Will you make more pancakes?"

"Yah, sure."

# Chapter Thirteen

RICHARDS BAY WAS two hundred miles further south. It was a full day's sail, though we sailed it mostly at night, a few miles offshore, with the hatch open and the stars above our heads. The stars hung so low it felt as though you could reach up and touch them. There were lights on the beach, too, where people were sitting around fires. It was a hauntingly beautiful night, and reminded me of how much I loved being at sea.

After a few hours showing Los how to run the systems of the sub, how to surface and submerge, and how the driveshaft hooked up to the engine, batteries, and stationary bike—things he already had experience with—I made a pot of tea and peeled three oranges while he sat on the bike and told me why I should stop burning diesel fuel. It wasn't something I expected to learn in Africa. I knew Africa only from geographic magazines. It seemed to me they showed only wars and famines, and kids without shoes or toys, running long distances to schools without books. I never expected to find someone like Los, who could design and build his own airplane, and who cared so much about saving the world that he was willing to risk his life for it. That was why he had made his flight—he was testing if a plane could fly without fossil fuels. He knew a lot more about global warming than I did, and was doing everything he could to solve the problem before it was too late.

"Vegetable fats burn just as well as diesel, Alfred. You just have to attach a converter to a diesel engine to make it work. You can't use a gas engine because the bores are too small. The fat builds up and clogs everything. I learned that the hard way. Burning fossil fuels, like diesel, or coal, throws carbon gasses into the atmosphere, and that makes the temperature of the Earth rise. Global warming is melting the ice in the Arctic and Antarctic, raising the level of the oceans, which are already starting to cover small islands and forcing people to move to higher ground. But millions of people will never be able to move because they have no money and nowhere to go."

He stopped to take a breath, but it was more like a gasp. "Carbon gasses also put more acid in the oceans, and that is killing the creatures who live there, especially the plankton, which produces half of the oxygen on earth. If we don't stop burning fossil fuels, we're going to destroy all life on this planet."

I handed Los an orange, and he ate it without even looking at it because he was concentrating so hard. I wondered if I had handed him a rotten apple if he would have noticed the difference. Probably not.

"Once we use up all of the fossil fuels though, there won't be any more to burn because they are not a renewable energy source. By the time that happens, it will be too late anyway. The oceans will be dead. Most of the creatures on the planet will be dead." He lifted his cup and took a drink of tea. "But vegetable fats are renewable. We grow them in our fields."

"But . . . doesn't burning vegetable fat put gasses into the atmosphere, too?"

"Yes, it does, but the carbon gas it makes is matched by the carbon that the vegetables take out of the atmosphere in order to grow in the first place. It's a fair trade. One evens out the other in the atmosphere."

"Oh."

We sat quietly for a while and drank our tea. Then we went outside. I was thinking about everything he had said. He wasn't the first person to tell me that the sea was dying. I had met an old man in the Arctic, an Inuit elder, who told me the same thing. He was passionate about it too, though he seemed to think it was already too late. Los was more than passionate;

he was trying to do something about it. He really wanted to save our planet. So did I; especially the oceans.

As I leaned against the hatch and watched for lights on the horizon, Los sat on the hull behind the portal, and dangled his feet over the side as we cut through the waves at eighteen knots. He was wearing the harness and a ten-foot rope. Now that his plane was well hidden, and we were on our way to South Africa, he was wearing a smile. He really was a likeable person, I thought, though not an easily likeable person. He was so committed to what he believed in, he didn't care if you liked him or not. I wasn't sure he cared that much about himself. If we were fighting in the trenches of the First World War, I was pretty sure that Los would be the first one over the wall to fight the enemy. My grandfather would have approved of that.

We passed three vessels coming from the other direction—large freighters, heavily loaded and low in the water—the first sign that South Africa, unlike Mozambique, was a developed industrial nation. As we watched the night pass, and chatted, we learned about each other's life.

Los was from Soweto, a township outside of Johannesburg, the biggest city in South Africa. He had been born and raised there, and went to school until he was fifteen. He spoke five languages: English, Afrikaans, Zulu, Swazi, and Sotho. But his mother died when he was fifteen, and he and his sister, Suzi, had to leave school then. He said he helped sell small sculptures, watches, and jewellery on the street corner for several years. But every night he went to a library in Johannesburg, studied books on science and mechanics, read magazines and newspapers, and went to lectures whenever they were offered. After his mother died, he looked after Suzi. They never knew their father.

We had a lot in common, except that my mother died when I was born, and I had met my father, and my sister, Angel, for the first time last year, in Montreal. Los said that he loved Soweto, his home, but that it was too dangerous for him to return.

"Why?"

He kicked at the water and hesitated. "Because of mob justice."

"What is mob justice?"

"It's when your community punishes you for committing a crime."

"Did you commit a crime?"

He shrugged. "Sort of. I didn't think of it as a crime at the time."

"But . . . why would your community punish you? Shouldn't it be the law?"

"It should be, but it isn't."

"Is it legal for your community to punish you?"

"No. But nobody cares what is legal. It doesn't stop anyone from doing anything."

"What about the police?"

"The police cannot do anything. There are too many people."

"How many people?"

"Three million, maybe four. No one knows for sure."

"They don't know how many people live there? Can't they count them?"

"Who would count them? Nobody cares how many people are there. Whole families live in little shacks. It is very crowded."

"How do they punish you?"

"They beat you until your muscles are like mush, until you are almost dead. Or they kill you. If they don't kill you, they often cripple you." His eyes shone in the dark. "They didn't catch me."

"But why would they beat *you*? What did you do that was so bad?"

"I stole something, just like you."

"I didn't . . . oh, yah, okay . . . what did you take?"

"A battery from a car. I didn't really steal it. I just borrowed it."

"Did you bring it back?"

"I was going to bring it back. Now, I can't."

"Why not?"

"Because it went to the bottom of the sea. Now, it is ruined."

"Oh."

"It wouldn't have been so bad except that the car was owned by Bandile Buthelezi. Of all the people in Soweto, I had to take *his* battery. I didn't know it was his car. He's so proud of his cars. That was unlucky. He is determined that I suffer mob justice, even if I don't deserve it. He has many connections. It is easy for him to get what he wants. I don't think they will kill me, but they will probably cripple me."

"That's horrible. What if you brought him a new battery? Would he forgive you?"

Los kicked at the water as if he were kicking at a soccer ball. "No. Buthelezi would never forgive anyone. He wanted to show off his car to people from another country, important people, and it wouldn't start. They laughed. He was embarrassed and ashamed. He would never forgive me. I can never go back while he is still there."

"But . . . what about your sister?"

"I haven't seen her for almost a year."

"That's too bad."

"She understands. She lives with a nice family. She knows I will try to see her when I can."

"Soweto sounds like a dangerous place to live."

"It is not somewhere you should ever go if you are a stranger. If you do, you must know people there, and you must know where you are, which neighbourhood you are in. There are no police to help you if you get lost or fall into trouble."

"Yah, that sounds dangerous."

"It is. But it is also the most famous township in the world. Nelson Mandela has a house in Soweto. So does Desmond Tutu. Their houses are on the same street. It is the only street in the world where two people have both won the Nobel Peace Prize."

"Cool. Are they rich houses?"

Los laughed. "No. The same as everybody else—plain houses. Mandela's house is a museum now."

"Wow. Didn't Nelson Mandela go to prison?"

Los spoke with deep respect. "For twenty-seven years. Then, when he came out, he became president of our country."

"That's amazing. That would never happen in Canada. A prisoner could never become the leader of the country. It would be impossible."

"But you never had Apartheid in Canada. In Canada, everyone is equal, right?"

"More or less. We still have rich and poor."

"Rich and poor is everywhere. Apartheid was inhumane and corrupt. Black people were treated like slaves, or worse, like animals. We couldn't leave our townships without special papers, or we would be beaten. We couldn't own good houses or have good jobs or go to good schools, or we would be beaten. We had no leadership in government, and no medical care. We had to live where the government told us to live, and take the worst jobs. And if we complained too much, we were beaten. The white leaders made sure we were always poor.

"But Nelson Mandela fought Apartheid to make South Africa free and equal for everyone. So, the leaders took him and threw him into jail, on Robben Island, where nobody can escape. But they could not stop him. Because you cannot kill the spirit of such a great man. It is impossible. And the rest of the world finally listened to Nelson Mandela, and they said, no, this must not continue; and the jaw of Apartheid lost its teeth. When I was a young boy, Nelson Mandela walked out of prison."

"He must be a brave man."

"He is the greatest hero of Africa. He is my hero. He has always been my inspiration."

"What about Desmond Tutu? What did he do?"

"He was the Archbishop of Cape Town. Now, he travels all over the world and fights poverty, AIDS and racism. He is a very great man, too. I am incredibly proud that the two most important people in Africa have houses where I was born."

He paused and kicked at the water rushing by his feet. "There is only one time that I can go back to Soweto."

"When?"

"When the national football comes to the big stadium."

"Football? What difference does that make?"

"The government built a huge stadium in Soweto. When national football is played there, everybody goes. Then the streets of Soweto are empty. Anyone can walk into Soweto then, take anything, and not be afraid of getting caught. But it doesn't happen often. Maybe a couple of times a year."

"It sounds kind of risky."

"It isn't. Everyone watches the football."

"Everyone?"

"Except for the oldest people."

"It must be crowded at the stadium."

"It is insanely crowded. There are so many people, you cannot breathe. The yelling will make you deaf for days. South

Africans love football more than anything else. Don't Canadians love football?"

"We like hockey more."

There was a splash in the water on the port side. Then another. Then a few more. I knew what they were. I recognized the sound. Los stood up. "What was that?"

"Dolphins. They love to follow ships. You'd better sit down. They'll jump right over your head."

Did they ever! And when they were in the air, we could see the light of the stars on their sides. I tried to count them, but there were too many. It was the biggest school of dolphins I had ever seen. There must have been hundreds. Los got excited. He started yelling loudly. "Weeeeeeeeeeeeeeeooohhhhh! Weeeeeeeeeeeeeeeooohhhhh!" Then he tried to touch the dolphins as they went over his head.

"You'd better sit down, Los."

"This is great!" He yelled at the top of his lungs as he tried to reach them. I ducked my head inside the portal to listen for the radar. I heard one dolphin splash very close to the sub. "Did you see that one, Los? . . . Los?" I raised my head, but he was gone. Oh boy. I jumped onto the hull, pulled on the rope, and helped him grab hold of a handle on the side. He was coughing up water.

"Los?"

"Yah."

"You've got to learn how to swim, man."

"Yah. I know."

# Chapter Fourteen

AFTER THE GENTLE green shores of Mozambique, where people lived in thatched huts and children played on the beach, Richards Bay was a shock. It had a large, deep-sea harbour, and was home to the largest coal-exporting plant in the world! Giant mounds of coal turned the south side of the harbour into a world of sooty blackness. They reminded me of the pyramids in Egypt, except they were black.

There were also factories and industrial yards here for aluminum, titanium, iron ore, granite, woodchips, paper pulp, and phosphoric acid, which, according to my guidebook, was used in batteries, rust remover, and soda pop. Freighters lined up in rows, like pack mules, waiting to carry the smelly stuff to factories all over the world. As we motored into the harbour at periscope depth, I had the feeling we were entering a hole in the earth, out of which all the materials of industry came. I couldn't help being fascinated, but Los wore a heavy frown. Coal was his enemy. Factories all over the world burned coal nonstop, spewing thousands of tons of carbon gasses into the atmosphere every day, heating up the planet and killing the oceans. And the biggest exporting plant for that coal was sitting right in front of us.

"I wish I could blow it up," said Los.

I wondered if he really would. I didn't think so.

There were nice areas of the harbour, too, with sailboats, deep-sea fishing boats, and even a pier of rescue vessels. That suggested there might be a real police force here, which was a welcome thought. But the harbour was enormous, and with so many corners and canals and piers, we spent most of the first day just looking for a suitable place to moor, and couldn't find one! Everything was too open and exposed. There was one channel that might have been a decent place to hide, but it was lined with sailboats, and had houses and condominiums right on the water. And it was only twenty feet deep. Someone was likely to see us sneaking in, like a snake in a drain pipe.

On the south side of the harbour, right in front of the monstrous coal mounds, were a few tiny coves that might be okay for hiding the sub at night, or for a few hours in the day, but I wouldn't feel safe leaving it there longer than that. If I did go with Los to Ladysmith, I had to expect to be gone for as long as a week. I couldn't leave the sub where someone might see it, even if the chances were slim.

We took turns steering around the harbour and staring through the periscope. Los wanted to practise diving and surfacing. But I had to stand next to him when he was pumping air into the tanks because, brilliant as he was, he was not very patient, and he brought us right up on top of the surface in the middle of the harbour, with a big show of bubbles and waves. I hit the dive switch immediately, and we went back down. Luckily, it was almost dark, and we could hope that nobody saw us. But by now, we were tired and hungry, and the crew was anxious to get out.

"There's got to be *somewhere* we can leave it, Alfred?"

"I don't know, maybe for now we should leave it in one of the coves in front of the coal."

Los frowned again.

"At least then we can get out and walk, and maybe find a pizza."

"Pizza?"

"Yah. That's the thing I miss the most at sea."

"Why don't you just make pancakes?"

"No way. I can eat pancakes whenever I like. I want pizza. And Hollie needs exercise. Just a minute." I went into the stern, dug out the South African money from underneath the potatoes, and brought it back. "Here's the money I took from the pirates. See how dirty it is? We have to wash it before we can spend it. Do you think there would be a laundromat here?"

Los' eyes opened wide when he saw the money. "That's a lot of money."

"I know. And it stinks, doesn't it?"

He covered his nose and nodded.

"But maybe we can buy a car with it. We have to clean it first, though. See the blood stains?"

He looked more closely. His face changed. He looked a little horrified. "People died for this."

"I know. I met one of them. Believe me, he wasn't very nice. Here. Let's wrap it in a towel and carry it in a bag. We'll take Hollie with us. Little Laura will have to stay behind."

I steered into one of the tiny coves and surfaced until the hatch was only two inches above the surface, just enough to climb out and not let water in. It took a lot of patience, care, and practice to surface so precisely, and I hoped Los was paying attention. It didn't look like it. His mind was somewhere else. I think he figured he knew how to submerge and surface now, and that was enough. It wasn't. Ziegfried would not have been impressed. He would probably have made Los practise surfacing every day for two weeks. And I knew what he would say to Los. "You can't go to sea in a submarine if you don't have patience." And he was right.

We slithered out onto the hull, up to our chests in water, and reached for the bank. I helped Los across. It was just five feet. Hollie swam it. Seaweed went up in the air. We climbed up the bank, stepped onto the railway tracks, and headed towards town. Our clothes dried along the way.

It was a warm and pleasant night. It was always warm and pleasant in Africa. We soon left the tracks for a road that led into the centre of town. The road took us through the woods, along the foot of the harbour, and past factories and industrial yards. There were *a lot* of industrial yards. Neighbourhoods had grown up around them. With so many smells to investigate, Hollie was thrilled with the hike, although he turned his nose up at some of the industrial smells. When we reached an area with streets and shops, and saw people on a corner, we stopped and asked if they could tell us where to find a pizzeria and a laundromat. Within half an hour, we were sitting at a counter, stuffing ourselves with pizza. Life was good.

The laundromat was harder to find. And Hollie was tired now. I had to carry him for a couple of miles. The laundromat was in a row of shops not well marked, but the people on the streets were friendly and gave us directions. There were two ladies inside the shop, waiting for their clothes to dry. They looked up when we came in and stared the whole time, which made it awkward to put the money inside the machine without them seeing it. They seemed awfully curious, probably because we were trying so hard to hide what we were washing. Our conversation likely didn't help, either.

"Won't this ruin it?" said Los.

"No. Not as long as we don't wash it for too long. I've washed some before by accident and it came out okay. And I've found some that had been in water for a long time, and it was fine once it dried. The thing is to use a gentle cycle on the machine. It will come out all yucky, but when we dry it, it will be like new."

"But won't the blood stain it? Blood stains clothing."

I glanced at the ladies and saw that they were listening to every word. Los didn't care. He didn't care two cents what other people thought.

"I don't know. I guess we'll find out. Oh. Shoot! We need coins. These machines don't take bills." I looked over at the ladies. Suddenly they turned away. I flipped through the money in the bag. Half of it was in one hundred rand bills; the other half was in two hundred rand bills. I was guessing there was about eight thousand dollars worth all together. We didn't know for sure. We didn't want to count it until it was clean. I pulled the cleanest one hundred rand bill I could find from the pile, walked over, and stood in front of the ladies. I waited for them to look up. They didn't want to, but eventually one of them did. "Do you think you could make change for us so we can do a wash?"

Both of them frowned. But one answered. "What do you want to wash?" I think they didn't have anything better to do than be nosy.

"Uhhh . . . a bunch of towels," I said.

The lady looked at Hollie, and she looked at the bill in my hand. She didn't believe me. "It's dirty."

I looked at the bill. At least it didn't have any blood on it. "I'm sorry. It's all that we have."

She made a face and looked like she wished I would go away. I stood and waited. Finally, she opened her purse. "Do you have any soap?"

"Oh. No. We forgot to bring soap. Do you think you could sell us some?" I asked nicely.

The other lady frowned even harder.

"Twenty rand," said the lady. "For the soap."

"Thank you," I said. "That's kind of you."

She gave me the change, and put some soap in a tissue. "What are you washing?" she asked again.

"Some towels," I said. I went back to the machine. While the ladies stared, we opened it up, pulled the towel carefully out of the bag, and put it inside the machine. Then we added the soap. I studied the directions, chose a delicate wash cycle, shut the door, and hit the button. We took two chairs, sat in front of the machine, and watched the money go around.

After fifteen minutes, the machine beeped loudly and startled us. We jumped up, opened the door, and looked inside. The towel was twisted up on the bottom, and the money was pasted all around the inside of the machine. Some of it was in thick wet clumps. It didn't look very good.

"Did we ruin it?" Los asked.

"I don't think so. We just need to dry it."

I handed Los the towel, then carefully peeled each bill from inside the machine and handed it to him. We kept our backs to the ladies so they couldn't see what we were doing, though they tried. Then we put the wet towel and money into a dryer, put in some coins, hit the button, and sat down.

It was warm in the laundromat and we were getting sleepy. Hollie curled up on the floor and shut his eyes. Los did the same thing on a chair. I tried to keep watch on the dryer, but my eyelids kept falling. Finally, we were shaken awake by the loud buzzer on the dryer. Los jumped to his feet, swung open the machine door, and out floated a few dozen crisp one hundred and two hundred rand bills. I turned towards the ladies, who were folding their clothes. They were staring at the money with a look of horror. I smiled awkwardly. "Oh! There it is. We found it. We didn't know where it was. It must have gotten mixed up in the towels." The ladies weren't listening. Now that they had seen the money, they couldn't pack their clothes fast enough to get away. How different it was here. In Canada, people would gather around if they saw money falling on the floor. In Africa, they seemed to run away from it. But we had little piracy in Canada, and an effective police force. Here, it was the opposite.

The money cleaned up fairly well, though some of it was definitely stained. And it was terribly wrinkled. We'd have to find a way to iron it, to flatten it. We stuffed it into the bag with the towel, and started back towards the coal dock. Now the walk seemed endless. We were dragging our feet. When we reached the sub, we hopped into the water, opened the hatch, climbed in, submerged to the bottom of the harbour, dried off with the towel, and went to sleep.

Tomorrow, we would buy a car.

# Chapter Fifteen

WE WERE WAITING for Los. He had gone to buy a car. He said that, if I came, the seller would see I was from another country, and expect twice the money. That made sense to me, so I stayed behind. But that was a long time ago. He should have been back already.

I was sitting on the grass above the train tracks, watching the sub and watching the harbour, trying to think of better places to hide. Hollie was lying beside me, chewing a stick, and stretching in a way he could never quite do inside the sub. Seaweed had been gone since yesterday, which was typical whenever we visited a new place. He was probably hanging out with other birds. He was a sociable bird. Little Laura was inside the sub, probably carrying small pieces of Hollie's rope and wood into her cage. Eventually, she would have enough to make a nest.

While I had made pancakes, Los had flattened out the rand by fitting it between metal plates, then pressing it in the vise in the stern. The money came out flat and crisp. Now, he was gone with the whole stash of it wrapped tightly in a rubber band, hidden inside a sock. For hours, I had been expecting him to show up with an old car. It felt like we had been waiting forever.

We had counted fifty thousand rand, give or take a couple of thousand. That was about ten thousand US dollars, or a little more in Canadian dollars. That was a lot of money in South Africa, especially to someone who didn't have any. The thought that maybe Los had taken the money and was never coming back kept sneaking into my head, and I had to chase it away. I trusted him. He was my friend now. Besides, it wasn't as though I had earned the money. I had stolen it. And the thieves and murderers I had stolen it from had surely stolen it from somebody else. Just because I had taken the money, didn't make it mine. It didn't make it Los', either. As I stared across the water and watched the freighters make the awkward turn at the mouth of the harbour and head out to sea, I wondered if I should have given Los just half of the money to buy the car. Why did I give him all of it?

A few more hours passed and it began to seem less likely that Los was returning. Now I started to worry that he had been seen with the money and robbed. What if he had been attacked and was lying in a field somewhere? Probably that hadn't happened. Nobody knew he was carrying it. He certainly didn't look like someone who would have money. And he wouldn't have walked around waving fifty thousand rand in people's faces. He was too smart to do that. I'm sure he would have separated a small amount from the bulk of it and gone looking for a good deal on the car. Probably he had to wait for a seller. Then, he had to test drive several cars, and negotiate. And then it probably took them forever to draw up a bill of sale. Yes, that would take some time.

But it was seven hours ago when he left, almost eight. That was a really long time. Maybe he had been told about a good deal out in the country, and had to walk there. I stood up, stretched, and danced around a bit to shake the stiffness out of my legs. We had been sitting on the ground all day. What if Los had simply bought the car hours ago, for five thousand rand, then realized he still had forty-five thousand rand in his pocket, no real connection to me, and no reason to come back, or not a good enough one? I began to wonder how long I would wait. It had been all day already. Twilight would be falling soon. Places that sold cars were most likely already closed.

I decided to wait until dark. If he wasn't back by then, I would know he had taken the money and gone and wasn't coming back. Maybe he didn't even buy a car with it. Maybe he just kept walking.

An hour after dark, I stood up again. I was trying not to feel like a fool. So I had waited one whole day? So what? So I had trusted someone with a bunch of money, and he took it? Big deal. It wasn't my money in the first place. And I learned a lesson: you can't always trust people. Sometimes your gut feeling is just wrong.

But we were friends. And the thought that a friend might have cheated me upset me. I tried not to let it, but it did. I realized now that I really believed in Los. I believed in everything he had told me about global warming and wanting to save the earth. He inspired me. It would be too disappointing to think that he had just been making it all up. He couldn't be. He had built and flown his own plane. He certainly wasn't making that up.

Then a car came by, and I, foolishly, got my hopes up. A few cars and trucks had passed during the day, but it was never him. Besides, I was waiting for the sight of an old car. All of the cars had been newer ones. It was time to go back to the sub. What was I waiting for?

And then . . . I heard the sound of a motorcycle. And I saw a motorcycle. And it had a sidecar. And it was Los.

I jumped to my feet. Los came off the road, over the train tracks, and right up the hill. Hollie jumped behind me. The motorbike was dirty, noisy and old-fashioned. But it seemed to run well. Los was beaming. "Alfred. Isn't it great? It runs perfect. It's got lots of power. See?" He revved up the motor until it roared. His eyes were wild and wet.

"I thought you were going to buy a car."

"Naaaaaah! A car wouldn't take us where we need to go. Jump in! I'll take you for a ride."

I looked closely at the sidecar. "Do you think it's safe? It won't fall apart?"

"Of course it's safe. You worry too much, Alfred. Jump in."

I picked up Hollie and climbed into the sidecar. I looked for a seat belt, but there wasn't one. There weren't any helmets, either. "Hold on, Hollie."

"Ready?"

"Okay. But don't go too fast, okay?"

Los put the bike in gear and off we went. It was always a shock to me how fast vehicles drove on land after I had been at sea. We went down the hill and onto the road. We drove to one end of the coal dock and back. Hollie stood up on my lap. He loved the wind in his face. "Don't go too far from the sub," I yelled over the noise of the engine.

"Hah! You are the captain of the submarine, Alfred. I am the captain of the motorbike!"

He turned onto another road and we were suddenly riding alongside an open-pit mine. Then, he made another turn and we were cutting through farms. Richards Bay had something of everything. On the way back to the water, we left the road altogether and drove across open ground. It was bumpy, but the motorbike seemed able to go anywhere. I could see now why he chose it. "How much did it cost?" I yelled.

"Ten thousand rand!" Los pulled the bag out of his shirt

and dropped it onto my lap. It was still full of money. He had bargained well.

"What took you so long?"

He looked at me, and then looked away. I think he didn't want to answer. But he did. "Because I'm black."

"Ohhhh."

"None of the car sellers would talk to me. Apartheid is over, but sometimes you wouldn't know it."

"Who sold it to you?"

"An old lady whose son died."

"Oh." Now I felt sorry I had doubted Los. And what if I had returned to the sub and left already? He would have learned he had been wrong to trust me. Thank heavens I had waited.

We rode the motorbike back to the pizzeria and bought three large pizzas. We ate one and took two with us for the next day. On our way back to the coal dock, I saw a gang on a street corner and, for a second, I thought they might be the pirates I had seen before. I wasn't sure. They weren't carrying knives or guns. But a chill went up my spine. Was it them? Would they hang around on a street corner in a place like this? They stared at us as we went by. But I was staring at them. Maybe I was just becoming paranoid.

We hid the bike in the bushes, not far from the sub. I took a careful look at the road with the binoculars. We were sure we hadn't been followed, but I wanted to check anyway. My gut feeling was nagging me now that I had seen those guys on the corner.

"Do you think that was them, Los?"

He shrugged. "I don't know. There are lots of gangs in South Africa. You can't tell who is bad and who is good just by looking, so you have to be really careful. Have you decided where to leave the sub?"

"Yah. I'm going to sink it."

"What?"

"It's the only way to leave it here and not worry about it. There's nowhere else to hide it."

"What do you mean, sink it? How can you sink it?"

"I'll set it on the bottom, climb out, and shut the hatch. Then, when we come back, I'll swim down, open the hatch, climb inside, and bring her back up. It's not the easiest thing in the world to do, but I've done it before. And it's one way that nobody will ever find it. I'll sink it right here in this little cove, where there's no current. It won't go anywhere."

"But . . . won't water rush in and flood the sub when you open the hatch under water?"

"Yes."

"But that's crazy."

"No, because I shut the hatch right away so only a couple of feet of water will get in, and the sump pumps will remove that in about fifteen minutes."

"But won't the sub come up to the surface then?"

"No, because I will let water into the tanks to keep it on the bottom. It won't surface until I pump air into the tanks."

"So . . . you will climb inside the submarine while it is flooding, and shut yourself in?"

"Yes."

"Okay, I thought I was crazy, but you are definitely more crazy than me."

"Maybe." Actually, I didn't think so.

We prepared for the trip before bed. I packed a can of fruit and some trail mix for Little Laura, some dog biscuits for Hollie, water, cookies, pizza, money, binoculars, a flashlight, and the tool bag I used for Hollie. This time, I was bringing it for Little Laura. I set the alarm so that we would rise an hour before the sun. Los lay down with the crew. I got cosy in my cot and listened to them shuffle and snore until I fell asleep.

Bright and early, we ate our last feed of pancakes and drank a pot of tea. I changed my t-shirt and shorts, brought the sub up near the surface, and took a good look around with the periscope before opening the hatch. Los made it to the bank himself with a big commotion in the water. He refused my help. Hollie swam it. I went back inside and coaxed Little Laura into the tool bag with a slice of peach from a can. Once she was inside, I closed the bag. It was a good carrier for her. She had lots of space, and felt protected. I carried her up the portal and swam her over to Los on the bank. Then I returned to the sub, grabbed the flashlight, pizza, money, and things, tossed them to Los, and asked him to hold the flashlight under the surface and point down. I shut the hatch, let water into the tanks, and submerged slowly, until the sub settled gently on the bottom.

It was sixty feet deep, which meant that the top of the hatch was a little less than fifty feet down. I always felt nervous when I had to open or close the sub under water because the water rushed in so powerfully and it took all of my strength to shut the hatch. I also had to do it while holding my breath. The whole action took only about eight seconds from the moment I started unsealing the hatch from the inside, to the moment I finished sealing it on the outside. The more times I did it, the faster I was. Still, it was unnerving.

Standing on the ladder, I tried to think if I had forgotten anything. No, I didn't think so. I took a few deep breaths, went through the order of what I had to do, then spun the hatch, pushed it up, and climbed out. Water flooded in with a weight like a house falling on me, except that it was a house that I was able to move inside. Even so, the force of it threatened to knock me down, and I had to hold on and climb out with all my strength. Once I was out, it wasn't hard to shut and seal the hatch. I turned, raised my head, and swam up towards the light.

# Chapter Sixteen

THE MOTORBIKE WAS made in Russia. It probably wasn't as old as it looked; it was just old-fashioned. It was noisy, tough, had tires like crocodile skin, and could climb any hill. The only thing I had to watch for was if we hit a bump unexpectedly. Then Hollie and Little Laura would go up in the air, and I'd have to grab them before they were tossed out of the sidecar. I rested my hands on them, just in case.

Hollie loved the motorbike. He stood on my lap and watched the countryside pass while he drooled on me. Little Laura seemed content in the tool bag, so long as she was close to Hollie. But we had to wait half an hour on the edge of town before Seaweed spotted us, flew down, and joined us. Waiting made me nervous because I had noticed an old car full of young men winding through the back streets of Richards Bay, as if looking for someone. I followed them with the binoculars as they made their way slowly in our direction. It was hard not to imagine pirates lurking around every corner. More likely, they were on the water somewhere, looking for the sub. In any case, I was relieved when my first mate finally dropped out of the sky and we could leave for the open country.

Seaweed didn't care for the bike because of the noise and bumps, but he would rest on the back of my seat when the road was smooth. I was a little worried there might be birds of prey in the South African sky, but I didn't see any, except for some small brown hawks. Seaweed probably looked like an eagle to them. He behaved like one, too. He had an extremely strong sense of self-importance and self-preservation. The only thing he was afraid of was snowy owls, and we wouldn't find any around here.

Los tended to drive the way a crow flies, cutting across plains whenever the road twisted too far in the wrong direction, or going over a hill instead of around it. I just assumed he was heading west, taking the shortest possible route to Ladysmith, but soon realized that the higher the sun rose, the more it fell on our backs. Either his sense of direction was terrible, or he was heading north on purpose. "Los!" I yelled finally.

He was lost in his thoughts and didn't answer for a while. "Yah?"

"Where are we going?"

"To Ladysmith."

"Yah, but why are we heading north?"

"Didn't you say you wanted to see elephants?"

"Yah."

"Well, we're taking a detour through the Umfolozi Reserve. It's not far."

"Oh. Okay. Thanks."

It wasn't easy to talk when we were riding. The engine was noisy, and so was the wind. I could tell that Los' mind was somewhere else, and he wasn't in the mood for talking. I didn't mind. I was happy to watch the grassy landscape go by. It was always interesting to spend time on land that wasn't surrounded by the sea. And I really did hope to see elephants, and maybe zebra and ostrich, too. I looked across the wide plain. This was Africa. It was pretty amazing.

For the first while, we didn't see anything but grass, bushes, sand, and rock. I had thought maybe Africa would look like India, but it didn't. It didn't feel like it, either. The air was drier, the light clearer, and the smells earthier. In India, the air smelled like water. In Africa, it smelled like the earth. If you imagined India as like a leopard, then South Africa was like a horse. Or maybe a zebra. And then, I saw one.

It stood in the field like a large pony. But it was as if some pranksters had come by with buckets of paint and painted black and white stripes all over it. "There's a zebra!" I yelled to Los. He just nodded his head a little. Then we went around a turn, and I saw three more. "There's three! Look, Los! Zebras!" But he just nodded again. He had obviously seen lots of zebras.

But there was something magical about them to me. And they were playful, like young deer, or dogs, running around the field chasing each other. A little while later, I saw what I thought were six bushes in a circle in the centre of a long field. Then, one of them moved, and I realized they were ostriches. "Los!" I yelled, and pointed.

"Watch this!" he said, and we left the road suddenly and raced across the field. He aimed straight for the ostriches. They raised their heads, saw us coming, and started to run. And man, could they run! Maybe on a smooth highway, at full speed, we might have caught them, maybe, but not on a bumpy field. We didn't even come close. Not only were they fast, they were huge. Their legs stood higher than my head. What a bizarre place this was, with black and white ponies, and birds as tall as moose. What would we see next?

Well, the next thing we saw was a large round stone in the middle of the road. It looked like a cauldron turned upside down. Los came to a sudden halt, and jumped off the bike. I climbed out, and so did Hollie. I looked at the stone, and I looked up at the sky. "Where did it come from?"

"It crawled here."

"Crawled here?" Hollie ran around the stone, sniffed it,

and gave a little bark. It wasn't a very convincing bark. I looked closer and saw a neck and face appear. It was a giant tortoise. The tortoise raised its head and gazed at me as if it were apologizing for blocking the road. It looked tired and old, as old as the world.

"We should lift it off the road," said Los. "It might get hit by a truck."

I looked around. There wasn't a soul in sight for miles and miles in every direction; and no sound except for the idling of the bike's engine. "What trucks would ever come through *here*?"

"Safari trucks."

"Oh." I stared at the tortoise. "Can it bite?"

"Yes. It can bite through your arm. And if it bites, it won't let go."

"Yikes."

"Don't let it bite you."

"I won't."

Los took one side of the tortoise, and I took the other. Carefully, we picked it up and carried it. It was extremely heavy, but we were able to move it off the road. It didn't seem to mind us moving it. I looked at the trail it had created behind it, and the ground in front of it. On both sides there was nothing but dry, dusty ground stretching endlessly. Where was it going? Where had it come from? I stared across the wide open landscape until it disappeared in a sunny haze on the horizon. Then I looked down and watched the tortoise move a few inches. There was such a sense of hopelessness about it.

But that was just my perception. This tortoise had been on the earth a heck of a lot longer than I had. And it knew where it was going and what it was doing. We were the ones who were searching. We were the ones who didn't know what we were doing. As I stared across the land, I felt a sudden guilt tear at my heart. We humans were threatening the whole world for every other creature. We had no right.

# Chapter Seventeen

BACK ON THE BIKE, we rode in silence for a long time. The vastness of the landscape was hypnotic. It was beautiful. It seemed so endless; it was hard to imagine that anything could ever hurt it. And yet, the land on the earth was smaller than the oceans. And what was bad for the oceans was bad for the land, because everything was connected. And I had already learned that the oceans were in trouble. Many people believed they had already started to die. Los was absolutely right; we *had* to stop polluting the earth before it was too late. But it was hard to imagine it being too late when you looked across a beautiful landscape like this.

After we rode through a dozen rolling hills, we entered a valley. Just over the crest of a small hill, Los coasted to a stop and shut off the bike. The air was silent and still, though my ears were ringing from the noise of the engine.

"I think we are in the Umfolozi Reserve now," said Los. "We better not get off the bike here in case there are lions. Keep your eyes open."

I didn't need to be told twice. We sat on the bike and stared across the valley. There were clusters of trees on both sides of a river. In the river, there were hippos. I watched them with the binoculars. They looked like fat grey cows with enormously fat heads. Los told me that hippos killed more people than lions did. They were extremely moody and aggressive, and they would attack you and drown you if you came near them in the river. Good to know.

Then, through the trees, came a family of the tallest creatures in the world. They appeared as if they had been waiting backstage to make an appearance. Like tall marionette puppets they stepped gracefully, and a bit stiffly, through the trees, though their heads were taller than the tree tops. They moved slowly and confidently. They made me think of dinosaurs. I tried to picture dinosaurs here, as they would have been so many millions of years ago. This was probably a jungle then, with rivers and swamps. But they were all gone now. Extinct. They died out and had been replaced by other species. Was that going to happen again? Were we about to lose the giraffes and zebras and ostriches, also the whales, sharks, dolphins, polar bears, and everything else? As hard as it was to believe, it was beginning to look like it. We had lost many species already. So many others were threatened. Why were we so destructive? What was it about human beings that made us this way? It didn't make any sense. If the world died, so would we.

But there were many people who weren't like that, who were trying to stop the effects of global warming, save the animals, and clean up the pollution. And Los was one of them. I wanted to be, too. As I watched a young giraffe run to catch up with its mother, I realized that this would be my last voyage purely for exploration. The purpose of my next one would be to do something active for the environment.

"We can't stay," said Los. "If the rangers see us, we'll be in trouble. If they think we are poachers, they'll chase us. They might shoot at us."

"Shoot at us? Okay, let's go. I don't feel like getting shot. It's bad enough being shot at by pirates. But I wish we had seen elephants. I wonder where they are."

"Elephants move around a lot. They could be anywhere."

Los started the motor. Suddenly, he stopped. "Alfred?"

"Yes?"

"Do you want to drive?"

"Drive? Uhhh . . . sure, why not?"

So, Los showed me how to work the gas, brake, and clutch. It wasn't so different from the sub in theory, but steering and balancing were, especially when it was bumpy. Sometimes the sidecar wheel would lift right off the ground. I started out slowly, practising braking and changing gears. It didn't take long to get the hang of it, and soon I was riding at about thirty miles an hour. It was fun, though I couldn't watch the scenery anymore because I had to keep my eyes on the road. After half an hour or so, I was feeling pretty confident. Riding a motorbike was a lot easier than I had expected. And then we came around the corner of a small hill, with a rock face on one side, and a sand dune on the other; and down the road in front of us was a small herd of elephants.

"Stop!" Los yelled. So I did. It took me just a few seconds. The elephants were standing on the road about three hundred feet away. One of them was a lot bigger than the others, and it had tusks. "That's the male," said Los. "The others are females. And there's a baby. We'd better be careful. Male elephants can be very aggressive when there's a baby around."

"What should we do? Turn around?"

"Yes. We'd better turn around."

"Okay." I was trying to remember the sequence of the gear shift, and the difference between the brake and the gas, when the male elephant started to run towards us.

"He's coming," said Los.

"I know."

"You'd better turn around now."

"I know. I'm trying to. I just . . ." Then I gave the engine too much gas; it bolted forward, then stalled.

"Hurry up!" said Los. "He's coming!"

The elephant came towards us like a train engine that started slowly, but was picking up speed. I started the motor again, put the bike in gear, and started to turn. But as the bike twisted around on the road, the engine wasn't responding to the throttle. Maybe the fuel line was pinched. It wasn't getting any gas. So, I turned the throttle up. Suddenly the bike shot across the road and into the sand dune. Hollie went flying off Los' lap, hit the sand, and rolled. The tool bag, with Little Laura inside, slammed into the bottom of the sidecar. Los held on tightly, but I went up and over the handlebars.

Los jumped out. "Run!"

I turned and looked for Hollie. He had picked himself up, but was covered with sand. I reached over and grabbed him. But what about Little Laura? What if the elephant crushed the bike? I had to grab her, too. So I reached into the sidecar for the tool bag.

"What are you doing, Alfred? Run! *Run!*"

The elephant roared. It was almost upon us. I could feel the weight of its steps coming up through the ground. But with Hollie and Little Laura in my arms I just couldn't get out of the way in time. Suddenly, Los jumped up, ran onto the road, waved his arms in front of the elephant, and yelled at the top of his lungs. The elephant didn't stop. It raised its trunk to strike him. Los turned around and ran. The elephant went after him. I dropped the tool bag and Hollie into the sidecar, pulled the bike around, kick-started it, and drove onto the road in the other direction. I turned my head to look for Los, but couldn't see him. The other elephants had left the road for the field.

A couple of hundred feet away, I stopped the bike and turned around. There, on top of the rock face, was Los, waving. I had no idea how he got up there so fast, except I suppose having an elephant chasing you could make you grow wings.

We waited until the elephants moved on, then I rode back and picked up Los. He had tears on the knees of his pants. He climbed in and we took off. A little further down the road, we parked the bike under a tree, sat down on the dry grass, and had some lunch. I brushed the sand from Hollie's fur, opened the tool bag, and let Little Laura out. She seemed okay, maybe a little shook up. Los pulled up his pant legs and examined his knees. He had cuts and scrapes but nothing serious.

"You saved us, Los. Thank you."

He shrugged. "It was nothing."

"Yes, it was. It was the bravest thing I ever saw."

He smiled and showed his teeth. "We're even. You saved me; I saved you."

"Yah, but I didn't risk my life to save you."

"But you would have, Alfred. I know it. Anyway, you wanted to see elephants. Now you have seen elephants." He grinned.

"Yup. I have."

I would have liked to believe that Los was right—that I would have risked my life to save him, too. But it seemed to me, you only know what you will do when the time comes. I had believed that Los would have been the first one out of the trenches to fight the enemy. He had just proved to me that I was right. He may have been impulsive and reckless, but he was the most courageous person I had ever met.

# Chapter Eighteen

WE ARRIVED IN LADYSMITH early in the evening. The sun was already falling on the Drakensberg Mountains. A soft, buttery light covered the trees, houses, and churches of the town. It was a pretty old town in a river valley. The river was dry, but was known to flood. There were mountains in the west and south, and hills in the east and north. The town sat in between them, and it was so pretty you would have thought it was a movie set.

Los pulled up in front of a small, plain white house with a steel roof and porch. The house was narrow in the front, but extended out in the back. There was a wooden picket fence all around, a backyard with trees, and a small barn. When he shut the motor off, the silence slowly began to replace the ringing in my head. Los stood up and stretched. I did the same. Hollie jumped out, trotted over to a tree, peed, and came back with a look of expectation on his face. I reached in and picked up the tool bag. Little Laura stared at me through the mesh. I stared back. I think she wanted out. "Just a tiny bit longer, Little Laura." I hung the bag over my shoulder and followed Los to the house. Seaweed dropped out of the sky and landed beside Hollie. "Hey, Seaweed. Nice to see you." He hopped onto the motorbike, spied the pizza box, and went looking for crusts.

Los rapped lightly on the screen door with his knuckles, and spoke with a much softer voice than I had heard him use before. "Katharina. It is Los. I have brought a friend."

There were sounds inside, and a shadow appeared behind the screen. As my eyes adjusted, the shadow grew into a dark-haired lady with bright shiny eyes and shiny teeth. She swung open the door with a great big smile, opened her arms wide, and wrapped them tightly around Los.

"My . . . dear . . . boy." It was a long hug. She didn't look at me until she let go. "And who is this?" She said *this* as if I had come from another world. I supposed I had.

"I'm Alfred. And this is Hollie." I pulled the tool bag out with my arm. "And this is Little Laura." I glanced over at Seaweed, but he had disappeared inside the sidecar. He didn't care for introductions.

Katharina smiled at Hollie and Little Laura, then took my

hand and squeezed it. I was surprised how strong she was. She gripped my hand tightly the way a labouring man would. Then she gave me a short hug, and it was as if someone had sat on me. "Come in!" she said, and disappeared inside the house. We followed her in.

Katharina was a special person. It was just as Los had said. She reminded me a lot of Sheba. Sheba lived on her own island, one of the tiniest islands in Bonavista Bay, Newfoundland. She lived in a house full of animals, birds, reptiles, and butterflies, and kept a hydroponic garden. I met her on my first voyage at sea, when I moored in her cove, thinking it was empty, and she discovered me, and thought I was a creature from the deep. Ever since then, she treated me like a son. Then she met Ziegfried, and it was love at first sight. Now they were married.

Sheba loved everyone, and everything, and was full of wisdom, dreams, and the ability to see into the future. Katharina was like that too, except that she didn't have animals of her own. All of the world was her family, she said. That's what Sheba would say, too. I didn't believe there could be another person in the world like Sheba, until I met Katharina. You would have thought they were sisters, even though they couldn't possibly have looked more different.

Sheba was tall and lean, with long, flowing red hair, and thousands of tiny, wave-like curls. She had bright green eyes, and when she fixed them on you, they had a power over you, warm and loving, but a power all the same.

Katharina was shorter and stockier—about my height. She also had long hair, but it was thick and black, and she braided it into tight, shiny coils that hung down straight, and held strings of colourful beads. Like Sheba, Katharina wore lots of jewellery, but it was thicker and heavier than Sheba's. Her limbs were smooth and muscular, like a gymnast, or a boxer. She always went barefoot. And her feet, like her grip, were tough. One thing that Katharina said really struck me. She told me she had been a witch in a former life. That wouldn't have startled me so much if Sheba hadn't said exactly the same thing. And that made me wonder if maybe they really had been sisters, somehow, in another life, if things really worked that way. I didn't know if they did.

Katharina's house was clean, tidy and bare. She didn't have much stuff. There was a wooden table in the kitchen, a few chairs, and in the living room there were cushions on the floor, but no sofa or bureaus or bookshelves. There were books, but they were piled neatly on the floor. There was music playing, but it sounded ancient. In another room, there was an exercise mat, weights, a pull-up bar on the wall, and a massage table. I wondered what she did for work.

"I'm an occupational therapist," she said, as if she had been reading my mind, which was probably true. "I'm also a yoga instructor, a personal trainer, and a dance instructor. I wear lots of hats. Mostly, I help people get better after an injury on the job." She looked at me. "Do you know this music?"

"I think maybe I heard it at another friend's house. You remind me of her."

"Do I? You must tell me about her. This is Hildegard von Bingen. She was a twelfth-century mystic and composer. Listen to how fresh her music is. You would think it had been written this morning."

"It sounds pretty old to me." I smiled.

"The instruments are old. The music is young. It's eternal."

"Cool."

Katharina grinned widely. She had nice teeth. "Yes, it is."

We had a great supper. Katharina cooked rice with vegetables, nuts, and tofu, and served pita bread, salsa, hummus, and tabouli. Los and I cut up the vegetables. It was not the kind of meal that Hollie got excited about. But there was fresh fruit, and Little Laura was very happy about that. She rode around the house on Hollie's back, which made Katharina bend over and laugh out loud. While we ate supper, we talked.

"So. Los. Where is your plane?" Katharina's voice was a little tough, too, but you could feel the warmth behind it.

Los raised his eyebrows but continued staring at his plate. I could tell he didn't really want to answer. "It sank to the bottom of the sea, but we raised it. Now, it is hidden on the ground, between some trees. I will borrow a truck and retrieve it. But it is in Mozambique."

Katharina was stunned. "No! You flew all the way to the sea? That is *very* far."

"I tried to turn around, but the air currents pushed me into the water. That's when I met Alfred. He was there in his submarine."

Katharina's mouth dropped open and she turned towards me. "You were in a submarine?"

"Yes."

She looked at both of us. "How can this be? One of you is in an airplane, the other is in a submarine, and you meet?"

We both took a bite, and nodded.

"If Alfred had not been there, I would have drowned."

Katharina stared at me with a serious face. "You saved his life?"

"Yes. But today Los saved my life by chasing away an elephant."

"I didn't chase it away. It ran away."

"He ran in front of it, and led it away. That saved us."

Katharina waved her hands in the air above her head as if she were dancing. "Hallelujah! You two were meant to meet. It is obvious you share a destiny."

Los made a serious face. "I would like to build a submarine, Katharina. Like Alfred has. That is why I have asked him to come here, to help me get started."

Katharina turned to me again and stared intensely, as if she were reading my face for clues. I wondered what she was thinking. "And do you think my Los can build a submarine like yours?"

"Umm . . . maybe. I'm not sure. It's a lot of work. It will take at least a couple of years. I just agreed to come and help look around for a suitable tank. I can't stay long."

"Where is your submarine now?"

"At Richards Bay. Under the water."

"Alfred is being followed by pirates," said Los.

Katharina continued to stare at me. I was starting to feel like a bug under a microscope. "Why are pirates chasing you?"

"I sank their boat, with drugs and guns on it. And I stole their money."

Katharina stood up, carried one dish over to the counter, and brought another one back. She was thinking hard, but maybe didn't want to share it. She turned to Los. "Could you make a submarine here?"

"If you would let me."

"Los. I would let you build a temple to Zarathustra here, if that's what you wanted to do."

"Thank you, my dear friend."

"You are welcome. What is troubling you?"

"I left my best tools in Soweto."

Katharina's face changed. She looked stiff now, and worried. "But you have many tools here."

"Yes, but the ones I need the most are in Soweto."

"But . . . you cannot go to Soweto, Los. You know that."

"I can go when the national football comes. Do you know when the next time will be?"

Katharina hesitated. She knew, but she didn't want to say. She answered so softly, we almost couldn't hear her. "Next week."

"Next week? That's great!"

"Is it?" She questioned him with her eyes. "Los?"

"Don't worry so much, Katharina. I will be careful."

Katharina didn't smile. She wasn't reassured at all.

"I *will* be careful. I promise you."

Her eyes fell onto the floor. She looked lost in thought, as if she were remembering something difficult. I had the feeling she wanted to say more, but wouldn't. She wouldn't interfere with his decisions. She wanted to, but respected him too much. I could tell it was difficult for her. Sheba would have been tougher with me. She would have fixed me with her stare, looked into my future, and tried to convince me to reconsider.

Maybe Katharina wanted to do that with Los. But he was older. And he was very stubborn. Besides, it was his decision to make. It was his life. And he had promised to be careful. Maybe that was enough. Maybe it wasn't so dangerous, after all.

After supper, Los showed me the barn. It was thirty feet long and fifteen feet high—just big enough for building a sub, if the sub were the same size as mine. But Ladysmith was a long way from the sea. You'd have to haul the sub on the road in the middle of the night, the way Ziegfried and I did, and launch early in the morning, to avoid getting a lot of unwanted attention. And you'd need a big truck and a special trailer. It was *so* much work. I didn't think Los knew what he was getting himself into. How could he? Still, I had to try to help. I would feel lousy if I didn't. And who knew anyway, maybe he could do it? After all, how many people could build their own plane, and fly it?

# Chapter Nineteen

WE SLEPT IN THE BARN. There was a wooden landing on one side where we put sleeping bags down and made ourselves comfortable. Hollie and Little Laura huddled together at the foot of my bag. Seaweed slept close by. I was tired, but these days, it seemed harder and harder for me to sleep on a surface that wasn't moving. And it didn't help that Los' snores echoed inside the barn like the wind inside a barrel, but it wasn't as nice as that. In the middle of night, I got up to pee. Hollie raised his head, but I shook mine, so he dropped his and stayed where he was.

I went into the backyard and stood between the trees. It

was a clear night. I stared up at the stars. This was Africa. The night sky spread out its stars differently here. The constellations were different, though I couldn't say exactly how. It made the sky look as foreign as the land, and the land was definitely foreign to me. I didn't know how to describe it except to say that it looked older than time, like the tortoise we had lifted off the road. It was dry, dusty, and tough.

Yet it was oddly full of humour, like the colours and shapes of its animals. And there was anger here, too, unless I had just been at the wrong place at the wrong time. I didn't think so. I remembered the elephant and the hippos. And I remembered the dead pirate. I remembered what he looked like, alive and dead, and the sound of his voice, and the stink of him. He had been filled with anger. And it finally brought him down, like a waterlogged boat. Sometimes, back home, a fisherman would leave his boat in the water too long. Then, one day, it would just sink. I remembered the sound of the scuffling that was his murder. I think I would always remember it. It was the sound of anger and hatred. It was hard to imagine it happening anywhere else. But I supposed it did. Of course it did. Then I remembered the coldness of his heart for locking Little Laura inside the sinking boat. That made me shudder for a moment, as warm as the night was. And then I heard a sound.

Katharina was in the backyard. She was down at the bottom of the fence, near the back of the barn. I didn't think she had seen me. She was looking up at the stars, too. On my way back to the barn, she saw me. She smiled warmly and came over. "You are not sleeping?"

"I just woke up. I'll go back to sleep."

She nodded. I bet she didn't say a lot of the things she was thinking. "You like Africa?"

"Yes. It's . . . different, that's for sure."

"How is it different?"

"I don't know; it's sort of serious and funny at the same time. I think I am just not used to it yet."

"I think you have already learned something very true about Africa."

"Maybe. I don't know."

"Let me ask you something."

"Okay."

"How is it you can ride your submarine all over the world like this, with dangers everywhere, and yet here you stand, fit, healthy, and ready to wake up to the next day full of life?"

Her question really surprised me. I didn't know how to answer it. I would have to think about it. "I don't know."

"I think I can tell you how."

"How?"

"You have an angel watching over you. I feel it."

"Really?"

"Yes. There is an energy around you. You have many adventures, but you always survive them, yes?"

"So far."

She reached out her hand for mine, so I gave it to her. This time, she didn't squeeze it; she held it gently. She turned it over, opened it, and pulled the palm of her hand slowly over the palm of mine. "You will live for a long time, Alfred. You will look out for many people. Many animals, too." She raised her eyes and stared at me through her dark braids and beads. Her eyes were warm, but I saw pain in them, too. "Will you look out for him?"

"Who? Los?"

"Yes. He is my peaceful warrior."

Peaceful warrior? That sounded like a contradiction to me. "What is a peaceful warrior?"

"Someone who is here to wage war against suffering and injustice and apathy."

"Like Nelson Mandela and Desmond Tutu?"

"Yes, like them. And like you. You are also a peaceful warrior, Alfred."

"I don't know about that."

"You are. I see it. But he ..." She tossed her head towards the barn. "He has already suffered more than you could ever know. It is a testament to the greatness of his spirit that he is still here, building, creating, dreaming, sharing. He has so much inside of him, so much love to share with all the world, if only he can escape his own demons."

"His demons?"

She stared deeply into my eyes, and I knew that she wasn't going to tell me any more than that.

"Does he not have an angel, too?"

Katharina smiled widely, and her teeth showed in the dark.

"He does." She looked serious again. "But his path is not as clear as yours. He shouldn't go to Soweto. It is too dangerous for him. But I cannot stop him. I know it. Sometimes, when we interfere with the journey of the ones we love, we cause them even more suffering without knowing it."

"Oh."

"Will you go with him?"

"To Soweto?" That sounded dangerous to me.

"I know you cannot protect him from every evil. But the angel that watches over you will watch over him also. Will you go with him?"

"I, uhh . . . I guess so. I have my crew, though."

"I will keep them safe for you."

I took a deep breath. "Is it as Los said it is—that everyone leaves Soweto when the national football comes?"

"Mostly everyone. He is right; it is the only time for him to go."

"Maybe I could go with him then."

Katharina nodded in the darkness as if we had just made a pact. Then, she took my hand again and pointed up into the sky. "There. Do you see those four stars?"

"Yes."

"That is the Southern Cross. You cannot see it in the northern hemisphere. Only here." She gripped my shoulder with her powerful hand, reached over, and planted a kiss on my cheek. "You will always be welcome in my home, Alfred." Then she returned to the house without a sound.

In the morning, we went out to explore the industrial yards around Ladysmith. Hollie and Little Laura stayed behind with Katharina, who was working at home. She said she had a client coming in, but that it would do her client a world of good to see a small parrot running around the house on the back of a small dog—a different kind of therapy.

Los and I took the motorbike out for a few hours. We tried a junkyard first, then the train yard. Then we snooped around a big tire factory, and then the hospital. There were tanks, for sure, but finding one that was twenty feet long, eight feet in diameter, without serious dents, not rusted out, free for the taking, or not too expensive to buy, was a challenge. They were not exactly lying around waiting for us. We tried riding past farms, small businesses, and a dump. After a few hours, Los was wearing a long face.

"Maybe you should put an ad in the paper, Los."

"An ad?"

"Yah. If you tell people what you're looking for, they'll call you. The tank you're looking for is probably out there somewhere, but we'll never find it because we don't know where it is. If people know that you're willing to pay for it, they might be willing to sell it, or, they might be happy for you to just take it off their hands, for free. But . . . Los?"

"What?"

"You're going to have to learn to weld."

"I know. I can cut metal with a torch already, but putting it together is different."

"Maybe you can take a course."

"Can't I just learn by myself?"

"No. Not welding. It's too dangerous."

I was starting to wonder if saying something was too dangerous to Los was like telling a bird that the sky was too high. "It's not only that it's dangerous. There are things you need to know so that it works right. If you don't weld it properly, your sub will fall apart."

His face grew even longer. "What if the course is too much money?"

"You can use the rest of the rand that I took from the pirates."

He looked surprised. "Really? You would let me?"

"Why not? It's not my money, anyway. And you're dedicated to helping the environment. I can't think of a better use for it."

His face brightened. "You are my true friend, Alfred. One day, we will both be in the sea with our submarines."

"I know. That will be awesome." Then I had another thought. "Maybe there's enough money that you won't need to go to Soweto for your other tools. Maybe you can just buy new ones here."

"No. I must go. I must have them."

Rats. I was hoping we wouldn't have to go. I didn't have a good feeling about it at all. I wondered if I should try harder to change his mind, but didn't know how. He was pretty stubborn. I supposed he had to be stubborn to get where he was. Still, sometimes there was a fine line between safe actions and unsafe ones, or, as my grandfather would say, between stubbornness and stupidity—my grandfather being the most stubborn person I had ever known. I had been learning about the necessity of safety ever since the day I first stepped into Ziegfried's junkyard. I seriously doubted Los ever gave it much thought.

# Chapter Twenty

WE LEFT FRIDAY, mid-morning. We didn't want to arrive in Soweto before noon. The middle of the afternoon would be best, when everyone was expected to be away. And we had to be gone by twilight, when people would begin to trickle back. By dark, there would be a mass movement of people in the streets. We had to be long gone by then, Katharina said, if we valued our lives. And I certainly valued mine.

It was two hundred and fifty miles. Soweto was on the southwest corner of Johannesburg. But we were coming from the south, so we wouldn't have to pass through the big city—one of the biggest and most dangerous cities in the world.

Even my guidebook advised avoiding Jo'burg if possible, and said that entering Soweto without a local guide was basically suicide. This wasn't a part of Africa I was keen to see. And I'd be glad when we had grabbed the tools and were on our way.

All the same, the road leading north was beautiful. There were mountains on the horizon, and rocky plateaus that reminded me of pictures of Nevada and Arizona—places I wanted to visit someday. There were zebras and ostriches too, but no elephants, giraffes, or hippos. It was very dry. And the further north we went, the drier it became, and the fewer animals we saw. I knew what Africa would become much further north because I had seen it before. I had ridden on the back of a camel into the Sahara Desert when we were in the Mediterranean a year and a half ago. The Sahara was a world that swallowed whole cities in sand.

We rode at a steady pace, not too fast. The bike developed a wobble if we went over fifty miles an hour. We stopped a few times to get out and stretch. Los knew the way, but I brought along a map for myself. It was so deeply ingrained in me to know where I was at all times, in terms of longitude and latitude, even on land, that I felt lost without it.

The closer we got to the giant metropolis, the more people we saw. At first, there were people walking alone along vast open stretches, especially women, carrying baskets on their heads. They walked where there were no towns, houses, or even trees. They walked under the direct glare of the sun, and never seemed to grow tired. But they must have been. It was hard to believe. You would never see such a thing in Canada.

Closer to the urban world, we saw small groups walking together, cars and buses. Now we began to see shanties in the open plain. You couldn't call them fields because there was hardly a blade of grass. It was so hot and dry. I was used to the heat now, after India and the Pacific, and yet it was intensified here in a way as we approached the city, that made it seem almost suffocating.

Finally, we saw signs for Johannesburg. Los made a sharp left turn, and we headed west towards Soweto. There were thousands of people along the streets and outskirts now Nobody here was watching football today. But this was not Soweto.

As we drew nearer to the township, the streets became quieter, which I took as a good sign. They never grew completely quiet, as I had expected, not even when we turned into the first neighbourhood beyond a sign that said SOWETO. Soweto stood for South Western Townships. It was an area of Johannesburg created when the leaders who started Apartheid forced all of the people who worked in the gold mines—black people—to live together in a community, away from all of the white people. I took a glance at the height of the sun as we entered. It was mid-afternoon.

Los rode rigidly, keeping his eyes straight, and not looking around. I couldn't help looking around; it was so interesting. It was extremely plain and poor. The houses were as small as houses could be, and there were thousands and thousands of them. They sat on rounded hills like an endless factory built out of individual blocks. There were very few trees, and just on certain streets. Some of the houses, as tiny as they were, had nice cars parked in front of them, which reminded me why Los shouldn't be here in the first place.

And there *were* people here, at least a few, on every street and corner. They watched us as we rode past. There were very few kids. The ones that we did see waved at us. The adults didn't. I just hoped that no one recognized Los, or, if they did, that we could grab the tools and get the heck out of here before they had time to come together and plan his punishment. I couldn't help feeling nervous. The thought of being beaten until all of our muscles were mush kept running through my mind. I could see why there would be no effective policing here. It was so vast, and there was such a sense of . . . I didn't know what else to call it except . . . desperation. Desperation with roots.

"Los. How much longer before we find the tools?"

He frowned tightly. "It's close!"

We rolled up and down the hills, riding deeper and deeper into the heart of Soweto. I looked for the sun, but it was behind me. It seemed to have fallen a lot in a short time. Finally, we slowed down on the crest of a hill, and Los veered off the road between some houses. Now we were on a dirt path with shanties, ditches, and garbage everywhere. It was filthy. I tried to get a sense of our direction in case I had to make my own way out, but it was impossible. There were too many twists and turns. Too many directions all looked the same. Suddenly Los came to a stop. I looked over and saw a long low shed with a rusty steel roof. The walls had been put together with pieces of wood, metal, and plastic. Along one side of it, on a long wooden bench, sat five men. They looked old and crippled. I saw their hands rise in the air when Los stepped from the bike. They recognized him. I knew that was a bad thing, but the men seemed friendly enough. No doubt they were too old to go and watch the football match.

Los crossed the yard and greeted the men in another language. He shook all of their hands, dropped his head, and spoke respectfully to them. They spoke respectfully back. They liked him. I could tell. He spoke to them for a few minutes, pointed to the bike, pointed to me, and then shook their hands once more. Then he turned around and motioned for me to follow him into a nearby shanty. I waved to the men, who waved back, and I followed him.

It was dark inside. The floor was just dirt. Los moved a bench out of the way, dug into the floor with his fingers until he found a piece of rope, and pulled on it. Up came a board, and underneath, was a hole in the ground. He reached down and pulled up an old blanket wrapped around something. He laid it down on the floor and opened it. As my eyes adjusted to the darkness inside the shanty, I saw a collection of wrenches, hand-drills, screwdrivers, punches, hammers, and chisels. They were nice old tools, but surely this was not all we had come for, risking our lives?

"Los. Tell me this is not why we have come here. Surely not just for this? We could find this anywhere."

He glanced up at me. He looked apologetic. "No," he said. "There is something else."

"What?"

"Someone I have to see."

I was starting to feel impatient. "Who?"

He paused.

"Who, Los? We've come all this way."

"I want to see my sister."

# Chapter Twenty-one

AS WE RACED THROUGH Soweto, with houses sliding by like brown shoeboxes, thousands of people began returning from the football match. They came up the sidewalks and streets in small and large groups. They were carrying blankets and laughing. Everyone turned to look at the motorbike with the sidecar. Lots of people waved. Many stared closely. A few times, the crowd was so thick that Los had to slow down, and I was afraid we'd get stopped, recognized, and beaten. I didn't know if they would beat me, too. I didn't know if they wouldn't.

"Try not to slow down, Los."

He nodded. I knew he knew. But I couldn't help saying it.

Finally, we reached a house. It was a red brick house. In Canada, it would hardly make a small garage. Here, it was one of the fancier homes. Los rode across the front lawn and stopped by the side door. He called inside, but didn't get off the bike, and didn't shut it off. A woman came to the door. She looked shocked and angry to see him. They spoke in another language. She was very angry. She pointed up the hill, in the direction we had just come, then waved anxiously for us to leave. Los dropped his head and nodded slowly. Then he turned the bike around and went back the way we had come.

"Los! Los! We have to go . . . now!"

He nodded, but kept going.

"Los!"

"They are trying to keep me from seeing her," he said. He was angry now. He wouldn't look at me. The streets were getting busier.

"Do you want to get us killed?"

He shook his head, but still wouldn't look at me.

We rode back towards the area where we had been, where the old men had sat on the bench. But we couldn't get close. There were too many people. We stopped in the middle of the street at the bottom of the hill. There was a crowd there, and several people were looking our way. I saw a group of young men who recognized Los. I saw them draw their thumbs across their necks. Los saw it too. I wondered: if I got out, could I make a run for it? I looked around. No way. Not a chance. There was nowhere to run. Everywhere was the same: tiny houses, thousands of people in the streets.

And then, just when I was afraid it was too late, Los put the bike in gear, dropped his head close to the handlebars, turned around, and rode away. He wound in and around the people, up and down the hills, out of the crowds, and out of Soweto.

I felt such a relief, my skin was tingling. We rode for about fifteen or twenty minutes, maybe ten miles or so. We left the highly populated areas altogether, and reached the open road that led back to Ladysmith. It was turning dark now. I was feeling the dry wind on my face, and counting our blessings, when Los rolled to a stop on the side of the road. "I have to pee," he said.

"Me too!" I had waited far too long.

"Why don't you go over there," he said. "And I will go here."

"Okay." I walked about thirty feet away, and stood behind a sign. Just as I finished, I heard the motorbike go into gear. "Los?" I came out from behind the sign and saw Los pulling away. He had turned the bike around and was heading back towards Soweto.

"Los!"

"I'll be back!" he yelled to me. "Wait here! I won't be lonnnnnnnnnnnn . . ."

"Los! . . . *Los*!"

He rode a few hundred feet, then stopped. Was he coming back? No. He waved something in the air at me, then threw it into the ditch. The money. I ran as fast as I could towards him, but it was too late. He was gone when I got there. I watched him disappear.

I jumped across the ditch and picked up the bag of money. What was I supposed to do now? Hitchhike? Start walking back to Ladysmith? It would take at least a week. Los had said to wait. I looked at the ground. It was almost dark. Yes, I could sit and wait, and hope that Los would make it back. But . . . I knew in my gut that he wasn't going to. I just knew it. No, I couldn't sit down. And I couldn't head towards Ladysmith.

So I started walking. I walked as quickly as I could, knowing I'd have to keep it up for two hours straight, at least. That's how long it would take me to reach Soweto, if I were lucky and could find it. I didn't have the map. It was in the sidecar. I didn't have anything, except the bag of money. I supposed I could watch for a taxi. In the meantime, I would just have to try to remember the way, and follow the signs.

I heard two voices inside of me: one, telling me to hurry— go faster and faster; and the other, telling me to turn around, get the heck out of here, and save myself. These two voices fought inside of me all the way. But I only ever stopped once, when I reached the sign that said SOWETO. I felt such a sickness in my stomach then. I felt I was abandoning all that Ziegfried had ever taught me about safety and making wise decisions. But the image of Los getting beaten by a gang of angry people kept coming into my mind, and I continued.

Yet, even as I hurried up the first hills, my limbs felt heavy, as if my hurrying were pointless, both for him and for me.

There weren't as many people in the streets now. Likely they were in their homes. Many were on the sidewalks though, and in front of their houses. There was a feeling of festivity in the air, though I couldn't enjoy it. It seemed false to me in a way, because of what I imagined was happening.

Then it occurred to me: what if Los had simply gone to visit with his sister, didn't get caught, and was now on his way back to pick me up? What would he think when I wasn't there? What would he do then? What if he was coming down one street while I was coming up another? I should have left him a note. Why hadn't I done that?

Because I knew in my heart that he wasn't coming back. Katharina's words ran through my head—I had to keep my guardian angel close to him, to protect him. But I guess I didn't really believe in guardian angels. I wanted to. I just didn't.

It was very dark now, and that worked in my favour because few people seemed to pay much attention to me at first. But the deeper into Soweto I went, the more they did, until, finally, they started calling out to me. Sometimes it was friendly, and sometimes it wasn't. When people waved, I waved and smiled back, but I couldn't hide the fear in my face. I had been walking fast for two and a half hours now, and was starting to feel I was going in circles. Where was the hill with the long shed and the old men? Then, suddenly, I ran into what I feared most. A gang of guys about my age saw me coming down the hill into the corner of their neighbourhood, and they came right over and stood in my way, stopping me from going any further.

"What are you doing here?" one demanded suspiciously. Another one was shaking his head in disbelief. I was in trouble.

I tried to speak without sounding afraid. I didn't really succeed. "I'm trying to find my friend. He's from here. He's in danger."

They laughed. "*He's* in danger? My friend, *you* are in danger. What do you think you are doing here? Do you even know where you are? Man, you are lost, aren't you?"

I took a deep breath. "Yes, I am lost, and I know I am in trouble. But my friend is in bigger trouble right now, and I've got to help him. Wouldn't you help your friend?"

The leader chewed on his fingernail. "What's your friend's name?"

"Los."

"Los who?"

"I don't know."

"You don't know?" They laughed again. "You come in here to save your friend, and you don't even know his last name?" He shook his head. "Why would you do that?"

"Because he's my friend. We met just a few weeks ago. I don't know his last name, but if I don't find him soon, they're going to hurt him really bad."

"Who's going to hurt him really bad?"

I hesitated for a moment, trying to take a quick look at each of them. I didn't know how they would react when I said it, so I said it quietly. "Mob justice."

It was as if I had spit poison. They took a step back. But the leader took a step closer. He raised his arm and dropped it on my shoulder. He pressed his face close to mine, spoke quietly, and pointed to another hill—a darker hill, with sparse lighting. It was a rougher area. I recognized it now. "Your friend is up there." He squeezed my shoulder, then let go.

"Thank you!" I said, and took off again. I ran to the hill. My lungs were dry and sore now. My feet were sore. But the worst was the sickness in my stomach from worry. A few more people came out to challenge me once I left the paved street and stepped onto the dirt, but I didn't stop. As I ran up the last hill, I had to jump over a few ditches with sewage in them. They stank terribly. I saw a wooden rack that was stacked with the gutted carcasses of cows. In the dim light I saw that the skin and muscles had been scraped from the bone, but the heads were there, and they looked ghastly. A cloud of flies hit me in the face.

I made it to the top of the hill and saw the long shed. The old men were still sitting there, though there were more of them now. I ran up to them and stopped, out of breath. I bent over because I thought I was going to be sick. When I raised my head, I saw two of the old men raise their hands and point, with very bony fingers, towards a larger shanty, about a hundred feet away. There was a small crowd outside of it. I nodded my head, thanked them, and headed towards the shed. As I neared the open door, the crowd moved to let me pass. Two men came out of the door. Then a third. They had horrible looks on their faces. They had blood on their hands.

# Chapter Twenty-two

LOS WAS LYING ON the dirt floor. He was unconscious. I was afraid to touch him because I didn't know how badly beaten he was, and didn't want to make it worse. I knew that if a person has an injury to the spine, they have to be moved very carefully. I bent down close and put my fingers near his mouth. He was still breathing. I felt his wrist. His pulse seemed normal, maybe a bit slow. When my fingers brushed against his face, they came away wet. Blood. But it was dark in the shanty. I couldn't see well. One thing I did know: he needed an ambulance. He had to go to the hospital *now*.

"Los. I'll be right back." I knew he couldn't hear me. I went outside. The small crowd had split up, and there were just a couple of people hanging around. They stared at me suspiciously. The old men still sat on the bench. I approached them. "I have to get an ambulance. Can you tell me how?"

The old men looked sympathetic, but shook their heads. I didn't know if they were shaking them because they didn't know how, or because they didn't speak English. I ran to another man. He had blood on his shirt. He had been involved in the beating. "Can you help me get an ambulance? Please?"

He shook his head furiously and walked away. He had understood me; he just wouldn't help. Then I saw a woman watching from the corner of the shed. She frowned and stared at the ground when she saw me coming. "It'll take at least three hours," she said angrily. "It might take five. You'd better get out of here now. They're gonna come back. They might beat him again. And if they do, you don't want to be here."

"If they beat him again, they will kill him. He's got to go to the hospital *now*."

She looked at me with such anger in her face, but I think she wasn't really angry. She was just feeling the same frustration and hopelessness I was feeling. "Child. Do you know where you are? This is Soweto. Soweto. It's gonna take you forever to get that boy to the hospital. And you know what you're gonna find when you get there?"

"What?"

"A twelve-hour wait."

"Twelve hours?"

"That's if he's lucky. Child, you are standing in the most violent community in the world." She pointed off in the distance. "That's the busiest hospital in the world. That's because people are killing each other every day, cutting each other up, and burning each other, and shooting each other, and beating each other. How many people do you think go there all cut up and shot and bleeding to death every day? Thousands! So, you can go call your ambulance, but it's gonna take them hours even to make their way up here. That's if they remember to come. What are you doin' here anyway? You don't belong here. How do you think you're even gonna get out of here?"

I didn't know what to do. There had to be a way to get Los to the hospital. I couldn't believe it would take twelve hours before he would get attention. I thought she was exaggerating. Surely once they saw that he was unconscious, they'd help him right away? On my way back to the shanty, I saw one of the old men get up from the bench. It took him a great effort just to get to his feet. His friends helped him, and they passed him a cane. He took a few steps in my direction and raised his hand towards me. I hurried over. He said something to me in another language and pointed across the way. It seemed urgent to him.

"What?" I said. "What is it?"

He kept pointing and urging.

"What? Something over there?"

He nodded and kept pointing. He wanted me to go over

there, so I did. I crossed the dirt yard and approached a couple of shanties. I looked back at the old man. "This one?" He
shook his head, but kept pointing. I turned to the next one.
"This one?" He nodded and called something out. I pulled
the door open a crack. It was dark inside, but I saw the glint
of something shiny. I pulled the door further. It was the motorbike. Yes! I turned and waved to the old man. I entered the
shanty, took the bike, rolled it under a hanging flap on the
back of the shanty, and ran it across the yard as fast as I could
and into the shanty where Los was. The old man sat back
down, but now he was making a quick sweeping gesture with
his hand. I knew what he was saying. He was saying, "Get out
of here, quick!" Someone else had probably laid claim to the
motorbike. They might think I was stealing it. We had to
leave immediately.

I didn't want to move Los, but had no choice. And there
was no one to help me. I ran to the door. The lady I had
spoken with was still leaning on the corner, watching. I waved
my arm to her to come. She didn't move. I waved again with
all the urgency I could show. Then I went back inside. I rolled
the bike next to Los. I couldn't get him inside without twist-
ing his body. It was terrible. And then, the lady appeared.
"Hurry up, child. Hurry up! They see you taking him away
and you are dead. They see me helping you and I am dead,
too."

"Please hold his head and shoulders as straight as you can,"
I said. "I will lift his body."

She stood behind him and lifted from under his arms. I stood over him and lifted straight up by holding on to the tops of his pants. He was so heavy. We just barely got him into the sidecar. I had to twist his legs sideways to get them inside. I thought I heard him moan when I did that, but I wasn't sure. We laid his head back, but there was nothing to hold it. Then she took off her sweater, rolled it up, and put it behind his neck. That helped. I took off my shirt and did the same. "Get out of here, child! Get out now, and never come back!"

I nodded. "Which way is the hospital?"

She pointed.

"Which direction? North, south, east, west? Which way?"

"North! Go!"

I started the motor. As we pulled away, I looked into her face and saw the fear in her eyes. I also saw the care. I reached out with my fingertips. She took them with her hand and squeezed them. "Go!" I would never forget her. I rode out of the shed, turned left, and went down the hill. As I looked back, I saw a couple of men running down the hill after us. I never stopped.

The Baragwanath Hospital was on the north edge of Soweto. The lady was right about that. I hoped she was wrong about the wait. It wasn't as hard to find as I thought it would be. There were signs and sirens. I followed both. The closer we drew, the more ambulances I saw. The sirens made me think of a city under attack, like London, England, in the Second World War. I didn't realize just how true this was, though it was a very different kind of war.

The hospital wasn't just one building; it was a maze of buildings. It was terribly confusing, but I followed the signs for Emergency, and they eventually took us there. What I saw gave me a terrible feeling that she had been right about the wait, too. Ambulances were unloading people onto the ground! This was because all of the stretchers were occupied. Horribly wounded people were lying on the ground outside, waiting for hours before even being taken inside. A small number of medical staff was going around, checking on them, trying to see who needed attention most desperately. From what I could see, they all did. So many people were cut, shot, burnt, or had smashed limbs and faces. It was the most horrible thing I had ever seen. At least one person appeared to be already dead. Still, no one could go inside the hospital. It was simply too busy.

I had to find help for Los. I climbed the curb with the bike, squeezed very slowly between people, many of whom were furious at me, and got close enough to a nurse to speak to her. "My friend has been beaten very badly. He is unconscious. Can you help us?"

She turned, raised her head, and glanced into the sidecar at Los. "Is he breathing on his own?"

"Yes."

"Then he can wait. Take your turn in line." She pointed to the people lying on the ground.

"But he might be bleeding inside. What if he dies?"

She was so busy, she didn't have time for my questions. "Do you see all these people?"

"Yes."

"Most of them are bleeding inside. Take your place in line." She turned away.

I called after her. "How long will it be?"

She shook her head and answered without looking back. "Ten hours. Fifteen ..."

I looked around. "Is there another hospital?"

A man sitting on the ground, with a bloody towel wrapped around his head, answered me. "No. They're all closed till morning. This is the only one."

I looked in every direction. Everywhere were people with terrible gashes, holes, and burns on their skin. It was a nightmare. I knew what I had to do now. I reached down and checked Los' breathing. He was still alive. I felt his pulse. It was slow. He had cuts on his face and head but wasn't bleeding as much as many of these other people. But he was very badly bruised. I doubted he could have opened his eyes even if he wanted to. I reached for the map, opened it, studied it, and put it away. I shifted Los' position to make him as stable as I possibly could. Then I turned the bike around, twisted our way through the wounded crowd, got back on the road, and headed south.

# Chapter Twenty-three

WE RODE THROUGH the night. The bike's headlight wasn't terribly strong, but the stars and moon helped light up the road. The road was empty otherwise. I stopped every half hour to check Los. He seemed the same, except that his face and hands had swollen. His whole body must have been swollen. Why had he taken such a risk? Would I have taken that risk to see my own sister? I thought it through. Yes, I probably would have.

His bleeding seemed to have stopped, at least the bleeding that I could see. But during one stop, I couldn't find his pulse, and I panicked for a second until I found it. It seemed weaker.

I wasn't sure. I would never have done this—taken him away from the hospital—if there had been any other way. The thought that he might die occurred to me. But what else could I do? He might have died outside the hospital. At least this way, I felt confident he would get medical attention in about five hours, instead of twelve. He moaned a few times, which I took as a good sign. Maybe he wasn't completely unconscious. But he must have been in horrible pain. I rode as fast as I dared, trying to keep the wobble from shaking the bike too much. I had to get us there without the bike breaking down.

Well, nothing broke, but two thirds of the way to Ladysmith, in the middle of nowhere, the engine sputtered a few times, coughed, and died. We rolled to a stop. "No!" I couldn't believe it. We had run out of gas. We filled the tank before we left Ladysmith, but I never thought to refill it before leaving Johannesburg. I was so used to running an engine with a tank that could cross an ocean. What now?

I looked behind us. We hadn't seen a town for a long time. Chances were we'd see one sooner the way we were going. There was nothing else to do but push the bike. And so I did. Thank heavens the road was flat. Within half a mile, I saw a light ahead. A mile beyond that, we came to a crossroads with an old garage and a few shacks. There was one light hanging from a pole. The garage was closed and no one was around. There was a gas pump, but it was locked. There was a truck in the yard that looked like it belonged to the government.

I went to all the shacks and banged on the doors. No one answered. I tried to pull the hose free from the pump, but the lock was three-quarter-inch steel. There was no way on earth I could break it. I had to get fuel. What could I do? What would Ziegfried do, I asked myself. Ziegfried would slow down and look at the problem logically, and solve it logically. Okay, I thought, I will do that. I stood and considered. There was gas in the pump and gas in the truck. I couldn't get into the pump. What about the truck?

I twisted off the fuel cap and took a sniff. Yes, there was definitely fuel in the truck. But I needed a hose. I ran around the yard looking, but couldn't find one. Then, I opened the hood of the truck. There were two long hoses that carried the wiper wash fluid from the tank to the window. I ripped them out, squeezed one end inside the other, and tied it tight with a wire I ripped free from the engine. Then, I sucked air through the hose to see if it would work. It did. So, I pulled the bike over to the truck, slipped one end of the hose into the fuel tank of the truck, put the other end into my mouth, and sucked as hard as I could.

It was really difficult, and the fumes made me sick. I had never siphoned gas before, only water. Each time that I had to stop, so that I wouldn't throw up, I pinched the hose, so that the fuel wouldn't fall back into the tank. Eventually, I sucked enough fuel into the hose that, when I turned it down into the tank of the bike, the gas flowed on its own current. It was only a trickle, but it didn't stop. And we had to make it only as far as Ladysmith.

As the fuel slowly ran into the motorbike's tank, I raised my head and looked around. This was theft. It would be terrible if I got caught. I had also sabotaged the truck. These were criminal acts. But what else could I do? I couldn't let Los lie around for twelve hours without medical attention, and I couldn't sit here and wait for the gas station to open. We were desperate. Desperation breeds violence, Los had said. Well, maybe sometimes it does and sometimes it doesn't. This wasn't violence. If anything, it was the opposite. Maybe sometimes you have to do something wrong to do something right. Los would have done the same thing for me. So would Ziegfried. So would my grandfather.

Just as the first shade of blue appeared in the sky, we reached the emergency wing of the hospital in Ladysmith. There was no one outside. There were no patients in the waiting room. There were no sirens or ambulances. It was quiet and still. The nurses on the night shift came outside with me, took one look at Los, and ran for a stretcher. After they took him away, they asked me to stay around and fill out papers. So I did. But as soon as I sat down and stared at the paper, I felt a terrible headache. I had just been through the most stressful day and night of my life. I was also dehydrated. My hand was so shaky I could barely hold the pen.

A few hours later, I rolled down the street where Katharina lived. She was standing on her porch when I pulled up in front of the house. She must have heard the bike coming. She had one arm wrapped around her belly and one hand on her face. She saw the blood on my clothes when I stepped from the bike. I suddenly felt exhausted when I saw her. Until now, I hadn't noticed how tired I was. It seemed to hit me all at once. Katharina looked strong standing there, bracing herself for whatever I had to tell her. "Is he alive?" she asked.

"Yes."

She came towards me and hugged me. I had to fight back my tears. Whenever would I learn not to cry, I wondered? Maybe never. Who cares?

"Will he be all right?" she asked hopefully.

"They don't know yet. He has a bad concussion. He has a lot of broken bones. It will take a long time to heal."

"But he will heal." She sounded determined.

I nodded. "Yes, he will heal."

"Is he here? In Ladysmith?" She sounded surprised.

"I had to bring him to the hospital here. I had no choice. We would still be waiting if we had stayed in Soweto."

Katharina shut her eyes. "You did right, Alfred. You did right. You must be tired now."

"I am."

"Come in. Get some sleep. I will go to the hospital. There is food in the kitchen. Please eat something."

"Thank you. Katharina?"

"Yes?"

"Los didn't go for the tools. He went for his sister."

"I know."

"But he didn't find her."

Katharina jumped into her car in her bare feet. "She was forbidden to see him."

"Why?"

"To punish him." She waved, and drove away. I went inside the house. There were cantaloupe, oranges, and strawberries on a plate. I picked up the plate and went into the backyard. Hollie, Seaweed, and Little Laura were there. I was so glad to see them. I sat down and shared the fruit with them. The older I got, and the more I learned about people, the more I realized that animals were better than people in many ways. I patted Hollie and looked into his sweet eyes. If every living creature had a heart like his, the world would be a happier place.

After half an hour, I put Hollie and Little Laura into the house, went into the barn, lay down on the sleeping bag, and fell asleep. I was dead to the world in seconds.

It was dark when I woke. Katharina was sitting in the kitchen with a cup of tea when I came inside the house. Hollie greeted me at the door. I was very surprised to see Little Laura sitting on Katharina's shoulder. She had never sat on my shoulder. She had never even come to my hand. I thought maybe she was afraid I might pull her under water again. I supposed she had good reason not to trust men. "She likes you."

"I dreamt about her."

"Really?"

"Yes. There was a woman on a boat, and she was calling out to me. Was there a woman in Little Laura's life?"

"Yes, I think so. I think her name was Maggie."

"Yes. That sounds right. Do you know what happened to her?"

"I'm not sure, but she might have been killed by a pirate. I'm pretty sure he stole her boat anyway. Did you really dream about her? That's pretty weird."

"It isn't weird at all. I do it all the time. I dreamt about you before I met you. Maggie is very worried about Little Laura."

"Oh. Is there any way to let her know that she is okay?"

"Maybe. If I dream of her again."

"Did you see Los?"

"Yes."

"How is he?"

"He has a bad concussion, as you said. He has swelling in his head, from bleeding. They will watch it closely. They might have to operate. They don't know yet. He has so many broken bones and bruised muscles."

"Is his spine okay?"

"It appears to be. If he comes through this . . ." She paused. "When he comes through this, he won't be crippled. But there is still a little concern for brain damage." She paused again. "Would you like some tea?"

"Yes, please."

Katharina made me a cup of mint tea and an avocado sandwich. I had eaten only a little fruit in two days. While I ate, she stared at her hands, and fiddled with her car keys. I could tell she was thinking about something she wasn't saying.

"Can you explain something to me?" I asked.

"I can try."

"Soweto was created to keep the black people who worked in the gold mines separate from white society, right?"

"Yes."

"And during Apartheid, the government used police to keep order there, right?"

"Order? I don't think you could call it order. It was a form of oppression."

"That's what I meant. But then, Nelson Mandela, and others, fought for freedom, and to end Apartheid. And they won. Right?"

"More or less."

"But the nurses at the hospital told me that there is more violence in South Africa today than ever before. And I saw it for myself. Why is that? Why, if the people have more freedom and opportunity, and less oppression, would they be more violent? Why didn't things get better?"

Katharina put her keys down and laid her hands flat on the table. "That's a good question. You're right. South Africa is more dangerous today than it ever was. Especially Johannesburg. And even more especially Soweto. I know that part of the reason is because there are more drugs around today. Drugs are a huge problem. People become violent, people who might never have been violent before. Drugs change their behaviour. It makes them very desperate."

"Doesn't poverty, too?"

"Yes, poverty does, too. But I think maybe drugs are even worse. It's a terrible combination anyway, drugs and poverty. But there *is* more freedom and there *is* more opportunity. And you see it. You see people getting ahead. But it's slow for most. Too slow. I think maybe real improvements in society take a long time. They don't happen overnight. And then, I also think that violence has been around for so long that it has become part of our culture. South Africa has the highest violent crime rate in the world. We have the highest rate of rape. We have the highest rate of AIDS. Did you know that a girl born in South Africa has a higher chance of being raped than learning to read?"

"Can that be true?"

"It is."

"I can't believe it."

"You must believe it, because it is true. Violence will be part of our culture until we have suffered long enough to do something about it. There are people trying very hard to change it, but there is a long way to go."

I watched Little Laura on Katharina's shoulder. She had been preening herself. Now, her head was tucked in against her feathers and she was falling asleep.

"She looks as if she is used to living with a woman."

Katharina turned her head and kissed the little bird. "She's a precious soul. I believe that Maggie spoke to me in my dream, Alfred. She is hoping I will look after her. Will you let her stay?"

I looked down at Hollie. He was curled up, asleep on the floor. It seemed a shame to separate the two of them; they had become good friends. Then I remembered Little Laura getting banged around inside the tool bag in the sidecar. Maybe she was too small and delicate for our travels. Maybe this was where she was meant to be. I looked at her again, nestled close to the dark braids and dangling beads of Katharina's hair. And I nodded.

"Thank you. I promise I will look after her very well."

"I know that you will."

# Chapter Twenty-four

THE LIST OF LOS' injuries was long. He had broken ribs, broken bones in his hands and feet, broken teeth, and a broken nose. There was a fracture in his neck, but the doctor said it was not a bad one, and would heal. He had blood in one lung, and his organs were bruised. His muscles had been pulverized. This was how you beat someone severely without killing him, said the doctor. The people who did it had experience, and knew what they were doing. This was mob justice.

It wasn't hard to understand *why* there was mob justice. If you had millions of people living in a small area, and no effective police force, you had to have some way to keep order. If you knew you would suffer punishment at the hands of your neighbours, then you might think twice before committing a crime against them. In some ways, it made sense that a whole community would choose the punishment together. Then everyone was taking responsibility for justice. It sort of sounded fair. I wondered what my grandfather would say about that.

What I didn't understand, was why anyone would beat someone almost to death for stealing a car battery. Wasn't the punishment way more than the crime deserved? If they had beaten Los any more, they would have killed him. That wasn't justice; that was just an excuse for violence. Maybe the people were taking out their anger and frustration by beating someone whenever they knew they could get away with it. Or, maybe it was even worse than that. Maybe they enjoyed it.

But that wasn't justice. And I didn't think that Nelson Mandela went to prison so that people could do that.

The swelling in Los' face was coming down with medication, and he was conscious now and could see. But he was doped up with painkillers and was very groggy. He couldn't speak. The swelling in his head had come down, too. That was the most important thing. They would watch him closely, but probably they wouldn't have to operate.

He would stay in the hospital for a long time though. And after that, he would stay with Katharina, in her house. It would be months before he'd be up and on his feet again.

Katharina told me I should go. I should say goodbye for now, and go. I could come back some day, but there was no point in staying here now. I knew that she was right, though it didn't feel good. I hated to leave Los like this, but I was worried about the sub. It had been sitting on the floor of the harbour for over a week. What if the pirates had gotten hold of a sonar device and were searching every harbour for it? I couldn't let them find it. And since there was nothing I could do for Los now, it was best to go.

I stood at the side of his bed, held his fingers gently, and stared into his swollen face. I hardly recognized him. "You're going to be all right now, my friend. Katharina will take good care of you."

He blinked and nodded ever so slightly. I knew he could hear and understand me.

"I'm leaving the money with Katharina. It's yours."

He shut his eyes.

"It's okay. I have more." I smiled. "I'm leaving the motor-bike too."

His eyes opened wider.

"You'll use it a lot more than I would. I'd probably just leave it on the bottom of the sea."

His eyes sparkled. I was pretty sure he was laughing inside.

"Listen, Los. I'm going to talk to Ziegfried. I will ask him if he will take you on as an apprentice for a while, so that you can learn how to build your own submarine, okay? I'll ask him, and will write to you here, at Katharina's. So, just get yourself better, and then maybe you can come to Canada and build your own sub, and then we will each have one, and can travel to places together, and watch each other's back. Okay?"

He blinked and nodded, and now he looked sad.

"Goodbye, my friend. For now. Goodbye." I squeezed his fingers gently, turned around, and went out. My heart was heavy.

Katharina thought I should take the motorbike, but I said no, I would have no use for it once I got to the sea. She said I could sell it. I said it belonged to Los now.

"But how will you get to Richards Bay?"

"I'll walk."

"Walk? It's over a hundred miles."

"I know. But I want to walk it. I want to walk and think. We haven't had a good hike for a long time. We'll enjoy it. It will only take us four or five days."

"But where will you sleep?"

"Under the stars."

"What will you eat?"

"I'll carry food and water. And we'll stop in Greytown. It's halfway. I only have to carry food and water till there. Do you have an old knapsack I can borrow? It might be a long time before you get it back."

"Yes. Take a sleeping bag, too."

"Thank you. Will you keep this for Los?" I handed her the bag.

"What is it?"

"Money. I took it from the pirates. We agreed that he would use it for his submarine. I might be able to send more. I will write to you, and him."

"Thank you, Alfred. This means more than you can know. I will keep it for him until he is better, and he will make good use of it."

"I know he will. Thank you."

We left with the sun the next morning. I wanted to get an early start, walk with an easy pace, and see how far we could get by dark. We said goodbye on Katharina's porch. She hugged me so tightly I felt I had squeezed into a wetsuit three sizes too small. I started to thank her for everything, but she put her fingers in front of my lips and stopped me. She smiled warmly, though I saw sadness in her eyes. "We will see each other again," she said. "I know it."

I believed her. I felt saddest for Hollie and Little Laura, who didn't know that this was goodbye. But it was the best thing for Little Laura. Whether Maggie had really called from beyond the grave or not, I think it was meant to be. Would Hollie and Little Laura remember each other when they met again? I was certain they would.

I carried fruit, nuts, bread, cheese, crackers, raisins, and water. I also carried the sleeping bag and a rolled-up mat. Katharina had insisted I wear an old hat. Later, I was glad that she had. I let Hollie walk as much as he wanted, and ride in the tool bag the rest of the time. Seaweed walked too sometimes, for short distances, but mostly flew ahead of us, then sat and waited by the side of the road until we came by. "Hello stranger," I would say to him every time we caught up to him.

We walked out of town and headed southeast. I felt mixed emotions. The full significance of what had happened to Los still hadn't settled in my mind. I was struggling with it. It had been so stressful finding him and getting him back to Ladysmith, so upsetting to see him hooked up to tubes in the hospital, unable to move or speak, that I never had the chance to deal with it. The injustice of the violence against him, especially when he was trying to save the planet and make it a better place for everyone, including the people who had beaten him, was hard to accept. He deserved so much better. So did the children of Soweto. So did children everywhere. They deserved a world without violence. Why were their parents robbing them of it?

After all of that stress, walking down an open road in Africa felt incredibly pleasant. It was so quiet, except for the sounds of birds and insects. And they made such unusual sounds, so different from anything I had ever heard before, that I wasn't sure which was which. It seemed to me that the winged creatures here made more musically rhythmical sounds, like drums and flutes, than anywhere else. The insects might have been lizards though, because I never actually saw them, I only heard them. And it wouldn't have surprised me if the birds were really people hiding behind rocks, playing flutes and gourds and drums. That's what they sounded like.

The sounds were a welcome distraction. They kept me

from dwelling too much on darker things, things I couldn't change. I kept an eye open for snakes, and reminded Hollie to do the same. He knew what they were. I didn't have to warn Seaweed.

We walked for a few hours, stopped, rested, and ate a snack. A few cars and trucks passed, and there were people walking in the other direction, towards Ladysmith. Mostly they were women with baskets on their heads. They smiled as they passed. The men we met crossed the road, shook my hand, rubbed my shoulder against theirs, and shook my hand again. This was a normal greeting. They made me feel welcome. Around midday, we found a tree with shade, rolled out the sleeping bag, and took a nap. We drifted to sleep to the song of an insect, or lizard, which sounded like someone winding up an old grandfather clock.

We woke in the middle of the afternoon, ate some oranges and crackers, drank water, and continued walking. Hollie was in his element. He trotted on the soft, spongy ground beside the road and smelled everything. He looked as if he couldn't believe his luck. By the end of the afternoon, I had finished recalling everything that had happened since Los and I first met. Now, I had to agree with Katharina that we had been destined to meet. It was too unlikely to have happened by chance.

When twilight fell, I began scouting for places to sleep. I didn't want to stay too close to the road, or too far away. I wanted to build a fire, but didn't want it seen from the road. I was a little nervous about elephants, but didn't think they would wander so far from a reserve. My guidebook said it was very unlikely they would. It was the same for lions and rhinos. I put a lot of faith in that book.

Funny how much more dangerous everything seems once it turns dark. In the night there were sounds we never heard in the day, strange wailing and screeching sounds, deep grunts, and a noise like someone blowing bubbles out of a long, hollow tube. I turned on the flashlight at least a dozen times during the night, but never saw a single thing. I chose a spot under a tree that I could climb. If any undesirable creature came by, that's where we'd be.

We slept lightly, beneath stars so brilliant you could almost see them with your eyes closed. Then we were up and walking before the sunrise, which appeared like a weak glowworm at first, then grew into an orange moth, stretched its wings across the sky, and lit up the sides of trees and rocks, casting long shadows. Then the sun came over the lip of the horizon like a ball of yellow fire, and I had to shield my eyes from it. Unlike the sea, the land lay perfectly still while the sun swept over it. And, unlike the sea, it was silent, except for the sound of our feet on the soft ground. There, on the road in front of us, I saw the shapes of women walking with baskets on their heads. Where had they come from? How did they just appear like that, as if out of nowhere? They must have been walking to Ladysmith, carrying things to sell. I wondered how they could walk so very far with such a weight on their heads, and never drop it.

But this morning was the most beautiful thing I had yet

seen in Africa. It filled me with awe, and hope. Maybe things were not as bad as I had thought. Maybe I had just been in the wrong places at the wrong times, or been unlucky.

No. I wished it had been that, but it wasn't. As I prepared myself to spend the day as I had spent the day before, contemplating violence on the earth, I passed one of the women coming from the other direction. She stared across the road at me and smiled. I smiled back. Her face was radiant in the sun. Without slowing down or breaking her rhythm in the slightest, she spoke to me. She said just three words. But those words buzzed around inside my head like a bumblebee for the rest of the day, blocking all other thoughts. "Appreciate your life," she said with a musical voice. As if she were singing a song.

# Chapter Twenty-five

HOLLIE AND I WALKED into Greytown just after dark on the second day. Seaweed was waiting for us. It was a smaller town than Ladysmith. On a quiet back street, which looked like it hadn't changed since the 1950s, we met an elderly couple, Edgar and Nancy. After a short conversation in front of their house, they invited us in for a cup of tea, which was very friendly of them, and reminded me of how people were back home in Newfoundland. So we went. Then, when they learned that we were sleeping under the stars, they insisted we stay for the night, and wouldn't take no for an answer.

Edgar and Nancy were the nicest people. They had lived in

Greytown most of their lives, and had seen many changes in their country, including the coming and going of Apartheid. It was interesting to listen to them, but I was terribly sleepy, and Hollie was comatose on the floor. He didn't even care that they had an old dog who was excited to have a visitor. Hollie just took one look at him, decided he wasn't a threat, flopped down on the kitchen floor, and went to sleep. I felt the same way, but they wanted to hear about my travels.

As the warm, soft air blew in through the open windows, and I sipped red-bush tea sweetened with honey, I told them. Usually, I didn't tell people about the sub, but this old couple was so friendly and curious that I just kept answering their questions until I pretty much told them everything. Soon I was *so* tired that I could hardly remember what I was saying. When they finally showed me to a room where I could sleep, I fell onto the bed with my clothes on, and never moved until the sun was up.

A large breakfast was waiting for us. Edgar and Nancy were dressed for travel. They explained to me that, right after breakfast, they were going to drive us to Richards Bay. They insisted upon doing it, and that's all there was to it. The road between Greytown and KwaDukuza was not as safe as between Greytown and Ladysmith, they said, and was particularly dangerous along the coast, between KwaDukuza and Richards Bay. As I didn't see how I could refuse, I accepted the ride.

I think maybe they wanted to see the sub, too.

Edgar wore a white cotton jacket zipped up to his neck,

and a grey cap. Nancy wore a yellow dress, a white hat, and carried a purse. She looked a little bit like the Queen. Edgar was tall. Nancy was short and round. I tried to imagine them much younger. They were the sweetest couple I ever met.

It was a little work getting the doors of the garage open and the car out. It coughed blue smoke when it started, showing that it hadn't been out for a while. Like its owners, the car was from a different age. They were excited when we all climbed in. I sat in the back, with Hollie on my lap. Seaweed rode on the roof. Edgar never went above thirty miles an hour. I watched the speedometer. But after walking for two days, it felt like we were in a race.

"Is that really your seagull?" Edgar asked.

I nodded. "His name is Seaweed." It was the third time he had asked me that. He just couldn't get his head around it.

"And he's going to climb into your submarine with you, is he?"

"Yes."

"And the dog, too?"

"Yes."

He stared at me in the rear-view mirror. His eyes were lit up. "Well, I have got to see that."

"Won't you be lonely at sea, Alfred?" said Nancy after a while. Her voice was high and squeaky.

"No, m'love," said Edgar. "He's got a crew." He nodded towards Hollie and the roof.

"Oh, yes."

I sat back and watched the scenery. I could hear the patter of Seaweed's feet on the roof. He was jumping off and landing. Nobody seemed to mind. Hollie was sticking his head out the window. I couldn't help wondering what Edgar and Nancy thought of Nelson Mandela. So I asked them.

"He was a good leader!" said Edgar loudly.

"He's a very nice man," said Nancy. She sounded genuine.

"He taught us a thing or two," said Edgar. "I must say, I was surprised."

"How so?"

"Well, I remember when Mandela was a young man. Things looked quite different then, you see. We thought he was a terrorist. He certainly was a militant. He went up north and learned all about guerilla tactics. Then he came back and stirred up all sorts of trouble. He was not like Mahatma Gandhi. Not at all. So we thought he was a violent man. I remember when he went to prison. And I thought to myself, well, that's probably where he belongs."

Edgar stared at me through the rear-view mirror, as if we were having a conversation across a table. I hoped he was watching the road. "Of course I was wrong about him. And Apartheid was a terrible abuse of power. That's a shame we live with now. I dare say we should have known better then. It was the way we were raised. My father thought that black people were monkeys."

He stared at me again. I think he was waiting for my reaction.

"That's crazy."

"Yes. It was crazy. It was real hatred. And it ran deep. You'll still find it in some places if you go looking for it. South Africa is a divided country. Always has been. Now it's more violent than ever. You might think it's the built-up anger, after all those years of being kept down. But that's not it. It's random, senseless acts of violence today, not aimed at any goal in particular. It's a hatred of a different kind. We've got a long road ahead. That's the name of his book, isn't it . . . what is it, love?"

"*Long Walk to Freedom*, dear."

"*Long Walk to Freedom*. That's it. Twenty-seven years behind bars! Then he became president of the country!" Edgar shook his head with disbelief. "You don't make that happen unless you've got something special in you. I think he did. He turned the country right around. We used to have two official languages. Now we have eleven! How many do we know, love?"

"Two, my dear."

"Two! Afrikaans and English. A long road ahead."

"*A Long Walk to Freedom*, dear."

"I know."

We drove in silence for a while. I stared out the window. I imagined sitting down at a table together with Edgar, Nancy, Los, and Katharina. I wondered what the conversation would be like. Then I tried to imagine Edgar's father. I pictured a mean, nasty, unfriendly, and unhappy man. Apartheid was born out of hatred. He would have believed in it completely.

We arrived at Richards Bay in the early afternoon. I warned Edgar and Nancy about the pirates, and suggested they drop me off on the outskirts of town, but they would not hear of it. Nothing was going to keep Edgar from seeing the sub. I told them to drive along the coal mounds. They knew where that was.

"Richards Bay is growing in leaps and bounds," said Edgar. "Used to be it was just gold in South Africa. And diamonds. Now, it's aluminum, titanium, and everything else. Look, here we are. Good Lord, it's three times what it used to be."

"My sub is in a tiny cove, over there." I pointed. I pulled the binoculars out of the bag and scanned the harbour.

"Any trouble out there?" said Edgar. He sounded ready for a fight.

"I hope not."

He parked the car on the side of the road and we climbed over the tracks and reached the bank. I saw them both stare at the empty water. I wondered if they thought for a moment that I was crazy, that I was just making it all up. I wouldn't blame them if they did.

"I'll have to swim down and bring it up. It could take about fifteen minutes. I have to pump out the water that will pour into it when I climb in. And that takes a little while. Don't be alarmed when I don't come right back up, okay?"

They both stared at the water with shock.

"Wait now!" said Edgar. "You're going to swim down there . . . how far is it?"

"Sixty feet."

"You're going to swim down sixty feet, climb in, pump out the water, and bring the whole machine to the surface?"

"Yes." I started breathing. "Will you keep an eye on Hollie for me?"

"We will indeed. Alfred?"

"Yes?"

"You know what you're doing, do you?"

"Yes."

"Okay then . . ." Edgar looked at his watch. "We'll see you in fifteen minutes."

"More or less."

I slipped into the water and went under. I heard Hollie bark as the water filled my ears. How glad I was to see my sub still lying there. When I reached it, I grabbed the wheel of the hatch and prepared myself. Every second mattered. If I made even a slight mistake, the sub would flood entirely and take much longer to empty, and I'd have to return to the surface to wait, and all of my things that I had hung out of water's reach would get soaked, except for the compartments in the stern, which were sealed. I focused my complete attention on what I was doing, spun the wheel, lifted the hatch, shoved myself inside with the water rushing in, stopped myself from falling by grabbing the ladder inside, pulled down the hatch, and sealed it. I was fast! Going in was faster than climbing out. I jumped down and found only a foot and a half of water inside. The sump pumps were running. I'd be on the surface in ten minutes.

I came up slowly, watching through the periscope as it broke the surface, just in case any vessel had come into the area while I was under. Edgar and Nancy were standing on the bank with Hollie and Seaweed. The coast was clear. I surfaced awash, with the portal just a couple of feet above. They would still be able to see the hull under water, standing so close to it. I opened the hatch.

They were staring as if an ugly monster had come up from the deep. In truth, the sub could have used a good scrubbing. Less than two weeks on the bottom of a warm harbour and all sorts of sea life had started to make their home on it. I particularly hated barnacles, because they would cut my skin when I was climbing on and off the hull, or even just sitting on it. I would have to find a secluded cove somewhere and give the hull a really good scrub. It would take a few days to do it properly. At the moment, the growth on the hull, plus the seaweed that got caught on the way up, and the dolphin nose that Ziegfried had welded to the front to make the sub faster, made the sub look like a living creature, or a dead one. Edgar and Nancy stared with their mouths hanging open.

"I guess I was faster," I said.

Edgar broke from his trance and stared at his watch. "Ten minutes."

"That's a submarine!" said Nancy, as if she were learning about it for the first time.

I swam to the bank and climbed up. "I'd better get going. There are people looking for me. I don't want to give them the chance to find me."

"Where will you go next?" Edgar asked.

"I'd like to sail around the Cape of Good Hope."

He shook his head. "You'll run into rough seas around the Cape, my son. That shore has been wrecking ships for hundreds of years. You'd better be awfully careful."

"I will."

"Drop us a postcard, will you? Sometime you're on shore. From anywhere. Just mail it to Nancy and Edgar in Greytown. The postman will know where to bring it."

"I will. Thank you for letting us stay at your house, and for feeding us."

"It was a pleasure," said Nancy.

"Any time," said Edgar. He shook my hand.

I held the bag over my head, slipped into the water, and swam to the sub. Hollie swam beside me. I carried him in, climbed out, and called Seaweed. He flew over, looked inside the portal, tapped his beak on the hatch, and dropped inside. Edgar and Nancy laughed and clapped from the bank. I waved. "Thank you!"

"Safe travels!" they called.

I pulled down the hatch and sealed it, went to the controls, and sat down. I let water into the tanks to sink a few more feet, then sailed out of the harbour like that. From mid-harbour, through the periscope, I saw Edgar and Nancy climb into their car. There was no one else around. The pirates weren't here. Had they given up? More likely, they were just searching somewhere else.

# Chapter Twenty-six

∽

I WAS WASHING money in the river—five-hundred and one-thousand naira bills, from Nigeria. It looked like more money than it probably was. We were sitting on the bank of a lovely river that emptied into the Indian Ocean somewhere along the southeast coast of South Africa. It was very beautiful. The coast grew more beautiful the further west we sailed—more rivers, more trees, more birds, more green and brown mountains close to the beach. This was a different world from inland South Africa, a different planet from Johannesburg.

There were blood spots all over the money still, and I couldn't seem to scrub them off. In fact, the harder I scrubbed, the bloodier they became. And then, the blood began to pour out of the holes and run into the river, and the river turned red. What was going on? Then, the pirate who had been murdered came walking up the beach. Blood poured from the holes in his clothes. What is going on, I asked? Nancy appeared. "Oh, let me take that into the kitchen where I can clean it properly," she said. I looked down at the money bleeding in my hands, but didn't want to give it to her. Then the woman from the road appeared across the river, smiled at me, and said: "Don't worry. Appreciate your life." And finally I knew, with enormous relief, that I was in a dream.

I woke on my cot in the sub. I raised my head and saw Hollie chewing on a stick, and Seaweed in a deep sleep. It was dark in the observation window. Now, I remembered. We were sitting on the bottom at three hundred feet. We were offshore from the Mkambati Nature Reserve. We had moored in a deserted cove and taken a long walk on a rocky beach. It had been windy and very beautiful. There had been a lot of strange-looking birds, and deer with horns that were twisted around like licorice sticks. It was an isolated corner of the coast. Most of the beaches we had passed in the Durban area either had people on them, or no place to moor the sub.

Just off shore from the Mkambati Reserve, was a sunken Portuguese galleon from the sixteenth century, lying in shallow water. I planned to look for it after breakfast, and practise diving there if I could find it. There were a lot of shipwrecks in South Africa. We had sailed over some already. I was pretty sure I had even found the outline of a submarine, on sonar. It was lying on the bottom at seven hundred feet, so we couldn't get close to it. It was probably a German sub from the First World War. There were lots of them in South African waters, resting on the bottom for almost a hundred years, their crews still inside. How I wished I could have seen one up close.

I made pancakes. That reminded me of Los. I wondered how he was doing now. Was he talking yet? Was he sitting up? As soon as I washed the rest of the African money, I would write to him and send it.

After breakfast, we rose to the surface. I took a look through the periscope before surfacing. It was clear. However, the moment the portal broke the surface, the radar started beeping. I glanced at the screen. There were three vessels offshore, about five miles out. That was no big deal; there had been lots of freighters and sailboats along the southern coast. But a small item caught my attention. It was probably nothing, just that two of the vessels were moving faster than the third, and appeared to be closing in on it from opposite directions, as if they were surrounding it. There were lots of things that could explain that, and it probably wasn't anything, but it gave me a funny feeling in my gut. What if it were the pirates, and they were attacking a sailboat, like Maggie's? I knew it probably wasn't that, but what if it were?

It wouldn't take long to find out.

So, I cranked up the engine and headed out to look. I already knew that two of the signals were just smaller boats, not ships, because they were moving so fast. Unless they were naval ships on exercise, which they could be, although I hadn't seen a single South African navy ship yet. And if they were, we would turn on our tail in a hurry. Likely they'd just think we were a local motorboat. They wouldn't know we were a submarine unless they saw us.

From three miles away, I stood on the portal with the binoculars and took a look. There were two outboard motorboats, similar to the ones I had seen the pirates use before. They had come from opposite directions to meet a larger inboard motorboat. Perhaps they were just fishermen out sport fishing. Or perhaps they were shark diving. My guidebook said it was popular here. Tourists went down in cages while bloody meat was dangled over the sides of a boat. It was one way to get into the middle of a shark-feeding frenzy without being the meal.

But the motorboats never seemed to actually meet the larger boat, only to come close. That seemed strange. Why would they keep a distance? Unless, maybe they weren't friendly?

Anyone watching on radar would know we were coming. That didn't bother me too much because we could disappear easily enough. But from two miles away, I switched to battery power, slipped beneath the surface, and approached at periscope depth. Now, we would have suddenly disappeared from their radar. Anyone paying attention would have found that strange. The last thing I saw before I sealed the hatch and went inside was the two motorboats spinning circles around the bigger boat.

From a mile and a half away, I thought I saw a flash of light through the periscope. It might have been the glare of the sun reflecting through the lens. We were approaching at eighteen knots, our fastest speed under water. They wouldn't know we were coming now unless they were staring at a sonar screen, which was extremely unlikely. None of the boats turned to meet us. But the two motorboats had stopped circling the other boat and were sitting in the water on opposite sides of it, about a hundred feet away. And then I saw the flash again. This time, I knew what it was. It was a rifle firing, from the boat in the centre. I turned the periscope to look at one of the smaller boats. It was the pirates! I was sure of it. There were six of them in the boat. It was them! They were heavily armed, and were shooting back. They were trying to seize the boat in the centre, but the crew was fighting back.

I looked at the boat on the other side. There were just two pirates on board. They were shooting, too, but not as much as they could have. They obviously wanted the boat, so they were trying not to fill it with holes. I scanned the boat in the centre more closely. I saw only one man in it. He was taking cover, and firing back whenever he could. He wasn't making it easy for them. I was glad. I wanted to help him.

We were close now. It was time to dive deeper, or steer away, or cut the power. I had to choose. But I hesitated. The pirates in the first boat moved closer, and fired into the cabin of the bigger boat. This time, the captain didn't fire back, and I wondered if he had been hit. I swung the periscope quickly to look at the other motorboat. They were firing, too. We were so close now. I had to make a decision.

I should have turned. It's what I would normally have done. But I didn't. I wanted to let them know we were here, that the captain in the centre was not alone. Then, maybe they would back off. Or maybe they would chase me instead, and the captain could head for shore, if he was able.

Two hundred feet away, and closing fast, I raised our nose and broke the surface with the portal. As soon as we had air, I hit the engine switch and cranked it up all the way. I wanted the extra power so that we could come in as fast as possible, and churn up the water in between the pirates and the centre boat. That would make it much more difficult for them to shoot straight. I aimed by looking through the periscope, then pulled it down at the last minute. I didn't want it to get damaged if they shot at us, which they were surely going to do.

But that is not what happened. Just at the time I figured we were passing between the two boats, I heard a terribly loud bang, and something struck the bow really hard. It shook the whole sub. It must have been a grenade. They must have seen us coming, after all, and threw the grenade just as we were passing. It was well-timed. I sure hoped it didn't cause us any serious damage.

No, it wasn't that. A couple of hundred feet beyond the boats, I climbed the portal, opened the hatch, and looked back. I couldn't believe what I saw. There, in the water, were pieces of the motorboat. It had been cut in two. All of the six pirates were in the water. They must have moved closer to the centre boat just as we came through. Had they not seen us coming at all?

My heart was racing. What if they couldn't swim? What if they were going to drown?

I swung around in an arc until we were approaching them again, then cut the engine, shut the batteries off, and scanned the water with the binoculars. As we drifted closer, I saw four men swimming or holding on to pieces of the boat. Where were the other two? I grabbed the lifebuoy, but was too far away to throw it. But I didn't want to move any closer, or the pirates would climb onto the hull and kill me. What should I do? What should I do?

Desperately, I grabbed the kayak, carried it up, and started inflating it. I thought I saw another man in the water now, but his head was down. Good Lord, what had I done?

The kayak was inflated in just a couple of minutes. I dropped it into the water and gave it a hard push towards the pirates. Then, I flung the lifebuoy with all my might, and it landed not too far away. They could grab it if they wanted to, to help their mates. But they never did. Two of the pirates took hold of the kayak and climbed in. The others still clung to pieces of the boat. I glanced at the centre boat and saw the captain wave. Then the other motorboat came speeding around from the other side. I ducked inside and pulled the hatch down. A bullet ricocheted off the portal. I sealed the hatch, climbed down, and submerged again. I went under the centre boat and up the other side. I surfaced, opened the hatch, and called to the captain of the larger boat. "Hey! Are you okay?"

He came out from hiding. He was holding his arm. "I'm okay," he yelled. "Just my arm. Thank you, my friend!"

"Can you sail?"

"No! The engine's buggered. Any chance you can tow me?"

I nodded. "Throw me a line."

He waved with his good arm, crept low along the cabin to the bow, and tied a towing rope. He did his best to toss the rope across the water. I motored closer. "Can you watch them while I tie the line?" I yelled.

"You bet!"

I climbed out with the gaff, grabbed the rope, and tied it quickly to a handle on the portal. I kept my head down and one eye on the other motorboat. It was a smaller boat than the one I had destroyed. They had picked up three other pirates, and now all five were staring into the water. I didn't know if they were searching for pieces of the boat, or for their guns, or for their mates. I counted seven men all together, with two in the kayak. There was one missing. At least they had stopped shooting, and were waving to the captain not to shoot them while they rescued their mates. He could easily have shot them now if he wanted to. I was glad he didn't. They would have.

"Should I ride with you?" he yelled.

I shook my head. I didn't know if I could trust him. I didn't trust anyone here. With his boat in tow, I headed towards shore. I kept an eye on the pirates as we pulled away from them. Now there were seven of them in the one boat, and they were heading off in the other direction. Their little boat was dangerously overloaded now. It was low in the water, in danger of capsizing. And they had my kayak in tow.

# Chapter Twenty-seven

I FELT AWFUL. I had killed somebody. I couldn't believe it. And I couldn't seem to make it better any way I looked at it. Yes, I had rescued Mickey. That was his name. He was a wreck diver. They would surely have killed him, and taken his boat, and all of his diving equipment, and sold it, and received money for it, and bought drugs and guns. But I had prevented them. And one of the pirates had drowned.

I wished I had done something differently. I wished I could have rescued Mickey without killing anyone. But there had been so little time. And I really didn't know what else I could have done. How could I have known they were going to move closer just when we came through?

Mickey didn't have any problem with it at all. He seemed glad the young pirate had died. We talked about it after I towed him to Port Edward. There was no pier there, so we both dropped anchor close to the beach. I pulled his towline taut and tied it to the portal. Then I jumped onto his boat. He shook my hand and gave me a hug, which was more like a pounding on my back. "Where in the Lord's name did you come from?" he said. "One minute, I'm a goner; the next, I see this creature come out of the deep and cut that boat in half. For a moment, I thought it was Divine Intervention. Hah! I am forever in your debt, my young friend. What's your name?"

"Alfred."

"Alfred. My name is Mickey. I'm from Cape Town. I'm a wreck diver. I've spent my life on these waters, and below them, but I've never seen a vessel like yours. Where do you hail from, Alfred?"

"Newfoundland."

"And where would *that* be?"

"It's in Canada. How is your arm?"

"Ahh, I've had worse. They just grazed the skin. A few stitches and a pint of rum and I'll be one hundred percent. The recipe: one part to the wound; ten parts to the belly. Hah, hah! You'll come into town with me?"

"I don't know. I don't think so. Those pirates have been chasing me ever since northern Mozambique. I thought I had lost them, but they'll follow me to the ends of the earth. I don't want to leave my sub alone."

"True enough. They chased you that long? There's only one reason for that. You took something of theirs, or you killed one of them."

"I killed one of them today."

"Nah! You never killed him at all. He done himself in the moment he joined that band of thieves and murderers. Good thing, too. Don't you carry that young fella's death on your conscience, Alfred, because it don't belong there. He died trying to rob and kill somebody, and don't you ever forget that!"

In my head, I knew that he was right. In my heart, I didn't. "They've been chasing me because I sank a boat of theirs. It was full of guns and drugs."

"Yah, I'd say that would do it. Are you sure you won't come in to town with me now? You look like you could use a drink, my son."

"I'm sorry. I guess I'd rather not. I think I need to spend some time alone. Thank you, though."

"I understand, my friend. I understand. But listen to me. You must go to the dock at Port Elizabeth. Go to one of the navy ships you see there. The harbour patrol boats, not the big one."

"The navy?"

"Yes, yes, the navy. They're terrific guys. My best friend is called François. You will find him on one of the patrol boats. Ask for him. Go and tell him everything you have seen of the pirates."

"Are you sure?"

"Yes, yes, of course. They are trying to catch them, you see.

They'll find your information helpful. The pirates never used to be so bold. Never used to come so far south. Now, they're in our backyard all the time. They're an awful menace, as you have seen firsthand. Go see François. Tell him that Mickey sent you."

"I don't know . . . I usually avoid police and navy vessels because I am not here legally. I never made a legal point of entry or had my passport stamped."

"Bahhhhhh! That means nothing to them. Just tell them that Mickey sent you. I will call ahead. They'll be waiting for you. I promise you. Will you trust me on this?"

I stared into his sunburnt and weathered face. He was wrinkled like an old potato. He looked wild, but honest enough. "I guess so."

"Good!" He touched his sore arm and winced. "I'd better go for my medicine." He gripped my shoulder with his good hand. "I will never forget you, young Alfred. I am in your debt for life. And I always pay my debts. You need something—anything—you call me, and I will do everything in my power to help you. You hear me?"

"Yes. Thank you."

"No, thank *you*. Safe travels, my friend."

"Safe travels."

Mickey climbed into a small dinghy and rowed to shore with his good arm. I waved. Then, I untied his tow line, tossed it onto his boat, climbed into the sub, and sailed away.

Sailing into Port Elizabeth was the very first time we ever sailed into a port on the surface, in the light of day, and didn't try to hide. It was such a strange feeling it made my toes curl. I flew the Canadian flag. I didn't have a South African one. From four miles out, I reached the port authority on short wave and told them who I was, and that I was supposed to meet a naval vessel on military business. That sounded so official, but I didn't know what else to say. I was told by a very severe lady to stay on the surface, and that I would be met by harbour officials. She sounded like the strictest teacher you'd ever likely meet, and it made me glad I wasn't in school anymore. I knew that, by the Law of the Sea, I only had to be on the surface when I was within the three-mile limit. But I obeyed anyway. The whole thing made me very nervous, and I stayed ready to flee if I saw anything I didn't like. I was trusting Mickey. I hoped that was right.

Port Elizabeth was a big city, with a wide harbour. I sailed in at a steady fifteen knots, giving them time to come out and meet me. But no one showed up until I was only a mile and a half from the dock. Then, two boats came racing out from different directions. I cut the engine, drifted to a stop, raised the binoculars, and watched them approach.

One boat looked as though it carried harbour officials. The other was navy. They arrived at the same time, although the navy boat had to race to catch up. As they reached me, I saw the naval officers wave the harbour officials away. "We've got this! We've got it! No worries!"

But the harbour officials didn't like that. They were insisting upon inspecting the sub. Then one of the naval officers jumped into the other boat and had a word with them. I heard him say something about it being a sensitive military matter, and that the harbour officials should stand down. They didn't like that at all, but they obeyed. The harbour boat turned around and went back. The two naval officers threw me a line. I tied it to a handle, and they jumped onto the hull.

"You must be Alfred," said one of them. He was a tall, tough-looking sailor with black curly hair. "I'm François. This is Major Richards."

"Tom," said the other man.

I shook their hands. They were both big tough guys, and I wouldn't want to mess with them.

"Mickey called me," said François. "Told me everything. Sounds like you've had quite the run-in with pirates."

"Yes. I have."

"Will you let us take a look at your sub, Alfred?" said Tom. "And your passport."

"Sure. I have a dog inside. And that seagull . . . there, is part of my crew, too." Seaweed had flown a short distance away when the boats came. He was sitting in the water, picking at his feathers. Both men looked at Seaweed and thought I was joking.

"This won't take long," said François. "It's just a formality, so we can say that we did it. And we'll return your passport." He looked apologetic. "Won't take long."

They followed me down the ladder. They had to bend their heads quite a lot once they were inside. "Well, isn't this something?" said François. "Here you go, Tom. Isn't this what you've been looking for?"

"It is indeed," said Tom, looking all around with curiosity. "This wouldn't do too badly at all. I might raise the ceiling a couple of inches. Can we see the engine, Alfred?"

"Sure. It's in the stern."

"You're a man after Tom's own heart, Alfred. He's been dreaming of a machine like this pretty much all of his life. Haven't you, Tom?"

Tom answered from inside the engine compartment. "I have. Come look at this, François. Look at the diesel he's got. Clean as my mother's table." He stuck his head out. "You should take care of the engines of our boats. How far have you come, Alfred?"

"Uhhh . . . well, I left Newfoundland last August. Then I came through the Northwest Passage . . . down through the Bering Strait, and into the Pacific. Then over to India. Then here."

François was beaming at Tom. He slapped him on the arm. "There you go, buddy. You're looking at your dream."

"Where did you build it?" said Tom.

"We built it in a junkyard in Newfoundland. My friend, who owns the junkyard, designed and built it. I helped him. It took us about two and a half years. A year after we launched it, we put the diesel in it. The first motor was a gas engine from a Volkswagen."

Tom nodded. He examined the batteries and driveshaft and nodded again. "It's a work of art. That's what it is. I'd say your friend knows a thing or two. He should come and build half a dozen of these for the South African navy. What we couldn't do with a few of these, hey?"

François opened the cold-storage compartment and peered in. I hoped he didn't lift up the potatoes. "Potatoes, Tom. All you need now is a side of beef, a dozen cases of beer, and you're set."

"Yah. And a couple of tuna fish and a grill. That's the life for me."

"Well . . ." said François, looking more serious, "I don't think there's any question of her being seaworthy. You've just come around the world. Mickey mentioned you sank a boat with guns and drugs, but I don't see any here. Have you got a rifle, hand gun, or weapon of any kind?"

"No. I have a flare gun, but I'm out of flares."

"Noted. And drugs? Did any of those drugs happen to stay on board this vessel by any chance?"

"No."

"No, you don't look like the sort of lad who would waste his life with that. Good for you. Will you follow us in, Alfred? We'd like to hear all you know about the pirates on the east coast. It's a serious problem for us now, and getting worse all the time. We'll set you up for the night, and fix up your passport for you. Mickey asked us to refurbish you with a few supplies, and we'd be more than happy to do that. If you let us throw a tow line around your hatch, you can follow us in at ten knots." He made an apologetic expression and winked. "It looks good if we tow you in. You understand, of course."

"Yes, I do. Thank you."

"A pleasure."

They climbed out, tossed me a line, and I tied it around the portal. Then they churned up the water with two powerful outboard motors on the back of their boat, and the rope snapped taut. I carried Hollie up, and we stood in the portal, and watched the harbour as we were towed in.

# Chapter Twenty-eight

FRANÇOIS AND TOM took Hollie and me out to a pub for supper, and we were served the biggest plate of fish and chips I had ever seen, and then a plate of apple pie and ice cream that we couldn't even finish. Hollie fell asleep on the bench before the meal was over, and my eyes were getting heavy. We weren't used to eating such large meals anymore. While we ate, I answered their questions about the pirates, and told them about everything, everything except the money and treasure. But the treasure came up anyway.

François and Tom were very committed to their job, and I respected them. They weren't stuffy and official, or afraid to bend the rules. They had families, played football, liked to fish, and were just regular guys who truly wanted to stop the piracy that was invading their country. So did I.

"The guy who was knifed by the pirates on Mozambique Island, I'm pretty sure we know who he was," said François. "His name was Jones."

"Yah," said Tom. "That's who he must have been. He was a really bad character."

"Mickey will be glad to hear he was killed," said François. "They had run-ins in the past. And Jones stole a treasure that Mickey had found in a wreck. It took him something like twenty-five years to find it."

"He found a treasure?"

"Yah. A few years ago. It was off one of the French islands . . . Europa, I think. The French took Mickey on board for questioning, and, while he was there, Jones raided his boat, took the treasure, and all his diving equipment, too. But Jones lived too dangerously for anyone's sake. It's no surprise to hear he was finally killed. He used to sell guns to the guerillas. Sounds like he was still doing that. That's pretty much a suicidal business in this part of the world. No doubt he sold drugs, too. You ran into some pretty tough characters, Alfred. You're lucky you're still here."

That reminded me of Katharina's belief that I had a guardian angel. I wondered if I did. "I know. How do you fight them?"

François took a deep breath. "Yah. That's the question.

After Apartheid, military funding was sharply cut, just like everything else. We don't have nearly the resources we need. But we do the best we can. We've got thirty harbour boats like the one you saw. We arm them when we need to. Then they're pretty formidable. We're moving some of our forces into Durban now. Buffing it up. That's where the biggest threat is. Mostly drugs. Pirates are all the way down the coast now. They get in with the locals, make them dependent upon them, and get them addicted to drugs. Then they control every aspect of their lives. The people live in fear."

"That's really terrible."

"It is. It's hard to fight, though. Up north, they attack freighters and tankers, take their crews hostage, and demand ransom. You see that on the news."

"I have."

"It's a battle we're waging. And we'll win. It'll just take time. But what about you, Alfred? I don't imagine you came here to fight pirates."

"No. I sure didn't. I'm just exploring. I've been exploring for more than two years now. But I want to become an environmentalist, and help protect the sea. I've seen some of the damage that's been done, and I want to help clean it up."

"Now *there's* a noble cause if I ever heard one," said François. "You've got my vote. Seems to me you're off to a good start."

"You should go to Australia," said Tom.

"Australia?"

"Yah. That's where the action is for environmentalism and the sea. That's where the Great Barrier Reef is, It's the largest reef system in the world. I visited there just two years ago. It's an awesome place. And it's *full* of environmentalists. If you want to get into the thick of active environmentalism, that's where you need to go. Tasmania, too. You won't find a more beautiful place, where people have been fighting for years to save the environment. And winning! Court cases in the papers, demonstrations, organizations going after whalers, that sort of thing. That's where I'd go if I were you."

He sounded like he wanted to go right now.

"How long would it take you to sail to Australia?" said François.

"I don't know. I never thought about it. I was planning to sail around the Cape of Good Hope and back home to Newfoundland."

"It's always good to go home," said François.

"I'd go to Australia," said Tom. "If I were in your shoes." He looked excited.

"You just want to travel in his submarine, Tom, that's what you want. Hah, hah!"

After supper, François and Tom showed us where we could stay for the night. Hollie and I slept in a room in a small barracks right on the dock. We were the only ones in the room. I was given a bunk bed, and there was a shower in the hall. It didn't matter that the bed wasn't moving; we were so tired. Hollie curled up by my feet. Seaweed was outside somewhere, maybe even sitting on the hull of the sub, because it was sitting on the surface and moored to the pier. The irony that we were being so well looked after by the navy, after hiding from navies and coastguards all over the world, was not lost on me as I drifted off to sleep. Funny, too, that it should happen in the most violent country in the world. Sometimes life was stranger than you could ever imagine it.

In the morning, François and Tom met us at the pier. I was happy to see that the sub was still there, moored between two navy harbour boats, as if it were part of the fleet. It was strange beyond words to see it tied up there. And I never had to worry about it because the pier was under constant surveillance. It almost felt like we were in the navy.

François and Tom drove onto the pier in a black pickup truck. They pulled out a bunch of supplies from the back. François had a stack of papers in his hand. "Okay, we got the paperwork done," he said. "Here's your passport. It's got a stamp. And here's a visa. You can come and go as much as you like. It's good for one year."

He handed me my passport. I opened it and saw the stamp, my very first one *ever*. There was a folded piece of paper stapled to another page. That was the visa. For the first time since I went to sea, two and a half years ago, I was actually travelling legally in another country.

"Wow! I can't believe it. Thank you so much! This is amazing."

"That's not all," said François. "We knew you didn't have papers for your sub, and so, here they are. Your sub is now officially registered in the city of Port Elizabeth, in the country of South Africa."

François handed me the registration papers. I stared at them and saw my name, a description of the sub, a serial number, an official stamp, and the South African flag. My mouth dropped. I really couldn't believe it. This was official documentation. I could present this anywhere.

"And here," said François, "is our flag." He handed me a shiny, brand new South African flag to fly from the portal.

I was really moved. "I don't know what to say. This is a really big thing. This will make my life so much better, I just cannot tell you. I can go through the Panama Canal now."

François stood with folded arms and smiled.

"And," said Tom, "we've got a South African navy issued rubber dinghy for you, an assortment of flares, a lifebuoy, some rope if you want it. And last, but not least, we're going to fill your tank with fuel, compliments of the South African navy, and our mutual friend, Mickey."

"Thank you so much," I said. "And that reminds me. I have something of Mickey's that I'd like to give you to give to him." I had decided this the moment I woke up.

"Sure thing. What would that be?"

"I'll have to get it out of the sub."

I climbed into the sub, gathered up my food tins, and carried them out. I put them down on the pier, opened them up, stuck my hands inside, and pulled out the plastic bags. François and Tom watched with confused faces.

"This was strapped to the bottom of Jones' dinghy after

the pirates had killed him. I didn't really know what to do with it, but I realize now that it should go back to the man who found it." I pulled the jewellery and gold coins out of the plastic bags and held them up. "Sorry my hands are all sticky."

"Good Lord!" said François. "Tom. Go give him a call. Won't he be thrilled to see this?"

"Will do. I'll be right back."

"Ahhh, you're going to make a happy man out of a good man today, Alfred. Mickey's put his life into finding this treasure. Lord knows he deserves it." He paused. "You could have just kept it. You really could have. But you didn't. Mickey said you were somebody worth helping out. And so we did as he asked us, because we owe him more good turns than I can count. But you didn't have to give this back to him, and you did. That says a lot about you, my friend. That says a lot. We are glad to know you."

"Thank you. I really appreciate your help."

François slapped me on the back. "It's nothing at all. You're practically one of us now."

I grinned. That didn't sound so bad.

# Chapter Twenty-nine

THE CAPE OF GOOD HOPE is where the Indian Ocean meets the Atlantic; where the warm water meets the cold. It isn't actually the most southerly point of Africa. That's Cape Agulhas, a hundred miles east. But the Cape of Good Hope is where sailors from the Atlantic stop sailing south, and turn east. It is the gateway to India.

The waters are wild here, and the sea floor is a jagged maze of rock, above and below the surface, making it one of the most treacherous coastlines in the world. If there were a ghost for every drowned sailor, then the shores of South Africa would be crowded with ghosts. I wondered if they were.

We sailed into the bay in the late morning. The sun was high and the day was clear, as it always seemed to be in Africa. There were lots of tourists on the sand and on the rocks above the beach. We sailed in on the surface, with the hatch wide open and the Canadian and South African flags flying side by side in the wind. I tossed the anchor a hundred and fifty feet from the beach, inflated our new navy dinghy, climbed in with Hollie, and paddled to the beach. Seaweed was on the sand already.

Several curious people came over to meet us, including a family with a whole bunch of young kids. The kids loved Hollie, and they loved the submarine. They asked me to bring it closer, but I told them I couldn't. It was too shallow. They asked me where I was from, and where I had been. We talked for quite a while. Then they took pictures with us at the sign that said *The Cape of Good Hope*. No one tried to steal the sub. No one tried to take the dinghy that I had hauled onto the beach. No one asked for my passport or looked like they were going to report us. There was nothing to report. It was wonderful.

But as I sat on the sand and watched Hollie run around with kids on the beach, I felt a terrible weight in my heart. I had been pulled into the violence that I despised so much. I had made a decision, taken an action, and a young man had drowned. He may have been a pirate, but he was a person all the same.

François said that if he hadn't died on that day, then he

would have died the next, or the day after that, or the day after that. It was a certainty that these pirates all die young, he said. Theirs is an impossible life. They have no life, no future. These boys have no future from the moment they are born.

I watched the kids playing with Hollie, and the kids being carried around by their mothers and fathers up the paths above the beach, and I wondered what kind of future they would have. Then, I remembered the face of the woman on the road, and what she had said to me, even though I hadn't said a word to her. "Appreciate your life," she had said. What bittersweet words they seemed right now, here, on this beautiful sand, on this beautiful day, with all these beautiful people around, while out there, somewhere in the choppy waters between the two currents, the body of a young pirate was drifting.

Later in the afternoon, we sailed into Simon's Town. It was a pretty town, right on the water, and was home to the South African navy. We came in with both flags waving. They knew we were coming. François had called on our behalf. We were given a berth right behind some tugboats. It was crowded. The navy was in port. It was thrilling to see the big ships up so close. Truly, this was one of the proudest moments of my life.

We moored in Simon's Town for three days and two nights. What a remarkable part of the world. There were more animals here, in the water and on the land, than I had ever seen anywhere. It was almost hard to believe. There were whales, dolphins, sharks, sea lions, seals, sea birds, and penguins in the water; and baboons, ostriches, zebra, deer, and penguins on the land. Hollie and I sat on the rocks and watched the penguins for hours. They lived a risky existence. They waddled around in the sun, jumped in and out of the water, but didn't swim too far from the rocks. The water was a dangerous place for a bird with no defences. We took a long walk in the hills, then along the water, and sat on the beach and just stared at the sea, because there was always something moving, jumping or gliding by.

There was also a marine museum, with relics from the war, and maps that showed all of the wrecks around the coast of South Africa, including submarines. There were a lot more than I had imagined. The museum was particularly interesting to me, and I could have spent the whole day inside. But Hollie's patience wore out. He stopped wagging his tail after an hour or two, and stared at every open window with such a longing look that I hurried through the last few exhibits and back out into the sunshine. Visiting Simon's Town was like visiting a zoo, an aquarium, and a museum all at the same time.

On our second day, Hollie and I took a train ride into Cape Town. It was a big city, but not as big, and not nearly as dangerous, as Johannesburg. We saw a township on the way in. Like Soweto, it had been very clearly planned out, and was separated from the rest of the city. There were wall-to-wall shanties stretching for miles and miles, blending into a dusty brown haze as far as the eye could see. High, chain-link fences surrounded the entire community. I didn't know if the fences were there to keep people out, or keep them in. The township ended abruptly, as if a line had been drawn in the sand. Beyond the fences was a new, beautiful and wealthy looking metropolis.

We hiked around the streets and waterfront for a few hours, then climbed Table Mountain, right in the centre. It rose high above the city, with a flat plateau on top, from which you could see far across the mountains and out to sea. It was extremely beautiful.

On the way up, we passed the homes of rich people. They were surrounded by high steel fences, with rolls upon rolls of barbed wire on top. Barbed wire surrounded schools, kindergartens and churches, too. Everywhere were signs promising quick-armed response to breaking and entering, and theft. Several of the homes looked like miniature fortresses, or prisons. How different they were from the shanties in the townships. It was hard to believe that people lived in both. When Edgar said that South Africa was a divided country, he wasn't exaggerating.

From the top of Table Mountain, I spotted an island offshore. I asked another hiker if it was Robben Island.

"Yes. That is it. You must see it. It is where Nelson Mandela was imprisoned. Now it is a museum. You must go see it."

"Thank you."

As I stood and stared at the island, clouds of fog appeared on the horizon. They came out of nowhere, and drifted into the bay with unbelievable speed. Twilight was falling. It was time to go. We climbed back down the mountain, bought a pizza, a bottle of chocolate milk, a bag of candy, and then caught the train back to Simon's Town. As I got comfortable in my seat, with Hollie on my lap, I stared out the window and smiled. Travelling legally had its advantages.

On our last day in South Africa, I went to a laundromat and washed the Nigerian naira and the rest of the American bills. The naira was equal to seven thousand Canadian dollars. I pressed all of the money in the vise, wrapped the naira in paper, and mailed it in a package to Katharina, with a letter for her, and one for Los. I kept the American money. I could think of no better use for it than to spend it on helping the environment. I then thanked the navy officials for their hospitality, climbed into the sub with my crew, raised both flags, and headed out to sea.

# Epilogue

ROBBEN ISLAND WAS cloaked in fog in the middle of the night. The island, the bay and the whole city of Cape Town were hidden in heavy fog. I had read that the waters off Cape Town were always rough. Were they ever! You couldn't drop anchor anywhere on the west side of the island. There was pounding surf, and the sea floor was impossibly rocky and jagged. The island was about five miles from the mainland. The water was cold, the waves high, and the current so strong it would carry away even the best distance swimmers. It was also full of sharks. This made it the perfect spot for a prison. No one who escaped the buildings had ever survived the swim.

On the east side was a breakwater where small ferry boats carried tourists over in the day. I steered into the man-made cove. There was no one there. My guidebook said that the prison where Nelson Mandela had been kept was close to the ferry dock. The whole island was only two miles long, but I didn't want to get lost wandering around and be here when the sun came up. I just wanted to have a look at the prison, and leave.

I left the crew inside, shut the hatch, tied up in a dark corner, climbed a rusty ladder, and stepped through the fog. It was dead quiet. I bet they didn't bother patrolling here at night. Who would ever come here?

It was spooky in the fog. It was spooky to think that this place had kept people imprisoned for hundreds of years. It had also been home to a leper colony. As I walked through the fog towards a long stone barracks with a light on one side, I wondered how Mandela felt when he was first brought here, and how he felt when he left. He came as a young man in chains. He left to become the leader of his country. Now, he was one of the most famous people of the twentieth century. But here, on this bleak rock, for more years than I had been alive, he had been a prisoner.

I was hoping there were windows, so I could peek inside with the flashlight. Well, there were, but the light didn't show through very well. I saw bars, and a blank wall, nothing else. Which cell was Mandela's? I knew it didn't make much difference, but I wanted to see it.

I went to the front. The door probably wouldn't be open, but I would try it anyway. Maybe they didn't bother to lock these buildings. To my surprise, the handle turned. I pulled open the door and slipped inside.

There was a long, dimly lit hall with evenly spaced doors on one side. The doors were made of bars. These were the cells. They were just small, plain rooms with enough space for a single bed and a small desk, nothing else. A sign in front of one of the cells said that it belonged to Nelson Mandela. I swung the flashlight inside, stood for a while, and stared. I tried to imagine the famous man sitting there on his bed, thinking about his friends and family that he could never see, sitting and watching his life slowly pass him by. He grew a lot older here, right here. Now, he was gone. I wondered how he had kept his sanity. How did he keep believing in what he believed? Could I have done that? No. No way. I couldn't. I would have been one of the ones who escaped and tried to swim for it. I'd like to think I would have made it.

There was a noise in another room. It sounded like a chair moving. Shoot! I didn't want to get caught. I shut the flashlight off and listened. Maybe I should run for it. I stopped breathing and listened carefully. I heard a light shuffling sound, like someone moving his feet on the floor. There was someone here, for sure, but they weren't moving much. Was it a guard? But there were no lights on, except for the weak lights above the doors. Who was here in the dark?

I crept down the hall towards a door on the left that opened into a large room. I stopped, shut my eyes, and listened. Some-one was breathing inside the room. "Hello?" I said quietly.

There was silence, and then . . . "Hello."

It was an old man's voice: rough, but quiet.

"What are you doing here?" I asked. I couldn't think of anything else to say.

"I live here. What are you doing here?"

"I'm visiting."

"You're visiting in the middle of the night?"

"Yes. I travel in a submarine. I didn't want to moor it in Cape Town in the day, but I wanted to see Nelson Mandela's prison, so I thought I'd take a look at night. I didn't expect it to be open."

"It isn't just Nelson Mandela's prison. Come in and sit down."

I came into the room. As my eyes adjusted to the darkness, I saw a small old man sitting on a chair on one side of the room. Except for a few chairs, the room was empty. I picked up another chair, put it down about ten feet away from him, and sat down. "My name is Alfred. I'm from Canada."

"I am Tony."

"Do you really live here?" For a split second it occurred to me he might be a ghost. He sort of looked like one. But he didn't sound like one.

"Yes, I live here. I have a small house. Many former prisoners have houses here."

"You were a prisoner here?"

"Yes. Now, I am a tour guide. Every day I lead people through here, talk to them, and tell them what it was like to be a prisoner here."

"Wow. That's cool. But . . . why are you here now, in the middle of the night?"

"I don't know. To remember, I guess. Sometimes, when I can't sleep, I like to come here. I like to sit in the dark and remember. In the day, it is too busy. Too many people. People come from all over the world. That is not how it was then. At night, in the dark, when no one is here, I can remember how it was."

"Why do you want to remember that?"

He hesitated. Then he laughed. "I don't know."

"Did you know Nelson Mandela?"

"Yes, very well. We were prisoners together. There were many other prisoners here. Nelson Mandela was just the most famous one. We have had many reunions since then, and he has come back often. But he is old now, and not so well. I haven't seen him for a while. Now, everyone wants to see Robben Island, because of him. Many famous people come here."

We sat silently in the dark for a few moments. His breathing was shallow, and I wondered if he was not well, either. I had lots of things to ask him, but struggled to find the right words. "Why . . . Don't you want to leave, and travel the world?"

"No."

"Really?"

"No. I never leave here."

"I think that would feel like being in prison to me."

He was quiet. And then, "That was one thing I learned while I was in prison."

"What was that?"

"That we carry our prison inside of us. If we no longer carry it inside, we are never in prison."

"I'm not sure I understand that."

"It is something you must think about for a long time. It took me many years to understand it. It was Nelson Mandela who taught me that."

"I will think about it. Can I ask you something else?"

"Ask."

"Do you know why South Africa is such a violent country?"

Tony was quiet for a long time. I could only hear his breathing. It sounded like he had asthma. I wondered how many nights he got up and came here. I was guessing it was often. He took so long to answer my question, I was starting to wonder if he had forgotten it, or maybe even fallen asleep. He hadn't. He took a deeper breath finally, and then . . . "No. I do not know why. South Africa is a violent country. Very many people are angry, for a very long time. I do not know why."

"Can I ask you something else?"

"Ask."

"Under Apartheid, South Africa was divided between white people and black people, right?"

"Right."

"And the white people controlled the government and army and police, and forced the black people to live in townships, and took away their rights, and kept them very poor, and without the opportunity for improving their lives, right?"

"Right."

"Well, can you tell me, did they do it because they hated the colour of their skin, or did they do it because of money?"

Tony was silent again for a long time. This time I knew he was not sleeping.

"You ask interesting questions. I think, when I was your age, all I wanted to do was play ball with my friends. A long time ago, I would have said it was because of the colour of our skin. But since then I have learned that people can forget the colour of a person's skin. It just takes a little education. But people never lose their fear of not having enough money. So, I would have to say that I believe Apartheid was more because of money than the colour of our skin. I think they used the colour of our skin as an excuse, but the biggest fear was the fear for the loss of money. People are more afraid to lose their money than they are to live across the road from people of different coloured skin. But what causes so much violence in our society? That I do not know. You give me much to think about."

"One person I met told me there would be violence here until people have suffered enough."

"Hmm. That is interesting, but I think that people will

always suffer, even after they have suffered enough. How much is enough suffering? Isn't any suffering too much suffering? I think maybe violence will stop only when people have more respect for each other. That is something I heard Nelson Mandela say."

"It sounds wise."

"He is a wise man."

"Thank you for answering my questions."

"You are welcome. And now I must get some sleep, or I will fall asleep tomorrow while I am talking to groups of people."

"Goodbye, Tony."

"Goodbye, Alfred." He laughed. "I thought you were a ghost."

"I wondered if you were. Have you ever seen ghosts here?"

"Oh yes. There are many ghosts here. It is a difficult place to leave."

I returned to the sub and motored out into the rising swells. I carried Hollie up and we leaned against the hatch together. Seaweed stood below us on the hull, pointing into the wind with his beak. The fog was lifting. There was the earliest hint of blue in the east. I reached up and felt the short stubble of hair on my head. It felt good. I stared north. The whole Atlantic lay ahead of us. It would bring us home. Then I turned and looked south. Just around the Cape, the Indian Ocean stretched all the way to Australia. It was the same distance in both directions. I felt butterflies in my stomach. I thought this decision had been made. Why was I hesitating?

I thought of Los, and wondered how he was doing. Was he sitting up yet? Was he talking? I bet he was designing his sub in his mind. That's what I would be doing.

I thought of Nelson Mandela. He would be waking soon, somewhere in South Africa, unless he was awake at night, too, like Tony. Mandela was an old man now. Most of his life was behind him. He must have been pleased with what he had accomplished. He had fought Apartheid and won. He was Los' hero. He was many people's hero. And now, he was my hero too, even though my fight would be a different one— for the health of the sea. I had a feeling that Mandela's answer for the violence that threatened his country—more respect for people—was the same for what threatened the whole world, only it was bigger—more respect for all living things.

I took a deep breath and scratched Hollie's ear. The butterflies were fluttering in my stomach. I steered to portside and cranked up the engine. As we rounded the Cape of Good Hope once more, the sun came over the mountains of South Africa and warmed our faces. I looked down at Hollie's eager eyes. I wondered if he missed Little Laura. If he did, he didn't show it. He looked like a dog on a mission. The sparkle of adventure in his eyes confirmed what I was feeling in my gut. "You're absolutely right, Hollie. Appreciate your life. We're going to Australia."

## ABOUT THE AUTHOR

Philip Roy resides in two places: his hometown, Antigonish, Nova Scotia, and his adopted town, St. Marys, Ontario. Continuing to write adventurous and historical young adult novels focusing on social, environmental, and global concerns, he is also excited to be presenting a picture book: *Mouse Tales*, the first volume in the *Happy the Pocket Mouse* series (Ronsdale Press), coming out in the new year. Along with the publication of *Seas of South Africa* this fall, Philip is bringing out the historical novel, *Me & Mr. Bell* (Cape Breton University Press). Besides writing, travelling, visiting schools, and running in the woods and countryside of Nova Scotia and Ontario, Philip spends his time composing music. His first score, for the Nova Scotia-based film, *The Seer*, by Gary Blackwood (FLAWed Productions) will be produced this year. Philip is also collaborating with Gary Blackwood on an opera, *The Mad Doctor*.